HUNT FOR MAGIC

DRAGON'S GIFT THE AMAZON BOOK 2

LINSEY HALL

CHAPTER ONE

I crouched on the rooftop, the night breeze blowing my hair back from my face. The sound of revelers echoed from the street below, but my attention was on the deadly race ahead. The whistle would blow any minute, and I wanted to be ready.

"You don't stand a chance," Lavender hissed at me from her spot ten feet away.

I didn't spare my fellow classmate and mortal annoyance a glance. Not that it shut her up.

"You've got barely any magic, and there's not a drop of water around here, so your only power is worthless. I don't know why you're even bothering."

Grim determination filled me.

I was bothering because we didn't have a choice. This race was one of the most important parts of my coursework at the Academy of Magic. Coursework was probably the wrong word for it, since most of it involved fighting and magic. But this time, we were racing across Edinburgh at night, in a magical game of capture the flag—from the top of Edinburgh Castle. There'd be dangers and demons in our path, of course, because nothing was ever easy at the Academy.

I had two goals: don't die, and don't make a fool of myself.

So, pretty much a normal day for me.

"The demons are going to make mincemeat of you." Lavender was really getting into the trash talk.

I shot her a sidelong glance. "I've never really had problems with demons. And I'm going to win."

There was supposed to be a big freaking prize for winning, and I wanted it.

She laughed, and I seethed.

Winning was unlikely, since she and the other competitors were totally in control of their magic and I wasn't. Not to mention, my new magic involved controlling water, and there weren't exactly any rivers nearby.

But I *hated* her smugness.

I shifted, eyeing the terrain ahead. Because the city was so old, the rooftops were different levels. I'd have to be fast, especially since it was me against Lavender, Angus, Carl, and Lorence—the other four students at the Academy of Magic at the Undercover Protectorate. I wouldn't put it past them to gang up on me, and I'd need to be ready.

I leaned over the edge of the building and peered into the alley behind me. My gaze caught on Jude, one of the trainers at the Undercover Protectorate's Academy of Magic. She was overseeing the race, and I wanted to impress her. Badly. If I did well, eventually I could join my sisters on her team, the Paranormal Investigative Team. Despite their ridiculous acronym—the PITs—it was the most elite team at the Protectorate.

I sucked in a deep breath and reminded myself of today's goals: stay alive, don't look like a fool.

If I could get a couple cheap shots in at Lavender while I was at it, I'd call it a win.

Before Lavender had a chance to hiss any more insults—

which I hated to admit were kind of working—Jude blew her whistle. The noise shrieked through the night.

I raced forward, sprinting as fast as I could. Strength and speed were the only things that would get me through this.

I sprinted across the rooftop, my feet silent on the old surface. Moonlight illuminated the Grassmarket, the supernatural district in Edinburgh. It was part of Old Town, and the buildings were ancient. The stone and brick structures were pressed cheek by jowl along the narrow streets and alleys, making for a fantastic obstacle course.

I used my speed to gain a few yards on my competitors. Their footsteps thundered behind me, sending my heart racing.

Run from the zombies.

I hated zombies, and pretending that Lavender was one gave me an extra burst of speed. She had all the charm of one, anyway.

When magic prickled in the air, the hair on my arms stood on end. I glanced back just in time to see an old metal trash can lid fly straight for me. Lavender's eyes gleamed with satisfaction.

The witch had used her telekinesis against me!

The trash can lid nearly slammed into my legs, but I was fast. I jumped over it, barely stumbling, and surged ahead. I darted around an unidentifiable metal structure and kept going, scrambling onto a higher rooftop as my competitors followed.

Magic swelled on the air again, and I was ready for it this time. A quick glance showed another trash can lid flying at me. It spun through the air like a giant frisbee, gleaming in the moonlight.

Where the heck was she getting so many?

As soon as it reached me, I jumped to avoid it but stumbled a little on the landing. The delay cost me my lead.

Lavender sprinted up to join me and breezed past as I caught my footing. I pushed ahead, lungs burning, and came up along-side her.

I almost missed the third object she sent at me. The old iron patio chair slammed into my legs, and I tumbled to the ground, skidding on the rough surface.

I looked up to see Lavender sprint ahead, followed closely by Angus, Carl, and Lorence. Blue magic swirled around Lorence's hand, and he shot a large icicle at Lavender. She was too fast, though, and dodged it right in time. Her laugh echoed over the rooftops.

My heart thundered, annoyance surging in my veins. I'd been through too much to go down like this.

I leapt to my feet and raced after them. Rage and determina-tion swelled inside me, giving me an extra jolt of speed as I sprinted across the rooftop.

We neared a section where an alley cut between us and the next building. The jump was long and dangerous. Maybe impossible.

Because they weren't stupid, my competitors veered right, taking a long way around that would definitely prove safer. An extension to the building at our right would give them safe crossing.

But it would take them longer to get there.

This was my chance to get ahead, if I was willing to take a risk.

Which, duh, I was.

I pushed myself faster, eyeing the wide gap between the buildings.

Could I jump that?

"Rowan! Don't even try it." Bree's voice crackled out of the comms charm tied around my neck. My sister was somewhere high in the sky, watching my progress. Technically, she probably wasn't supposed to talk to me during the competition, but she'd never been one for rules.

I ignored her warning and pushed myself faster. I was almost there, and I would need a good burst of speed to make the jump.

"It's too dangerous!"

I ignored Bree and sucked in a deep breath, sprinting faster as I neared the gap. I was nearly to it when I realized how damned wide it was.

Ah, shit.

But then, big risks were the only way to win when you had wonky magic like mine. At least no one would say I'd lost because I'd wimped out.

My heart thundered as I leapt, pushing off the ground with all my strength and sailing over the narrow alley. The wind tore at my hair and my stomach plunged as the ground opened up below me.

It was *so* far down.

Holy fates, I wasn't going to make it!

The jump was too big.

A scream caught in my throat as I reached out, fingertips stretching. They scraped against the edge of the building, not catching hold.

I reached with my other hand, scrambling for purchase. I caught the sill of the top window, my arms jerking as my weight dragged me down.

Sweating, I clung to the windowsill, legs dangling. My skin chilled in my ears as I registered a newfound fear of heights.

Yep, I was now officially a little afraid of heights.

"You moron!" Bree's voice sounded through my comms charm, but I was pretty sure I could hear her from above too.

Still dangling, I glanced up, catching sight of my sister's silver wings as she darted down toward me, ready to save me.

"I've got this!" I gasped. "Back off!"

I'd be disqualified if my mega-powerful sister jumped in to save me. Not to mention totally embarrassed. I loved her enough that I didn't mind living in her shadow. But if she rescued me from my own dumb decision in this race?

I'd never live it down.

"Still a moron," Bree muttered, but I could hear the love in her voice, twined with a little bit of admiration.

I clung to it, using it as fuel for my aching muscles as I pulled myself up the side of the building. The toe of my black leather boot found a notch in the old stone wall, and I pushed upward, hand over hand until I reached the top of the building and hauled myself over.

Lavender and the others had nearly reached me by now, so I'd lost a lot of my lead. But since I wasn't yet dead or totally embarrassed, I was still *technically* winning.

Adrenaline made my legs shake as I pushed forward, sprinting across the rooftop to try to keep my lead. I had a few yards on them, and I sure as heck wasn't going to lose it.

There was another jump ahead, this one much narrower, and I sailed across with ease. As I flew over the gap in the buildings, I caught sight of a gleam in the alley down below.

Water.

The liquid moved sluggishly through the alley, either from a broken pipe or some kind of drainage. But damned if I wouldn't use it. The others were behind me still, so it was perfect.

I reached out with my new magic, grateful to finally have some power of my own after so long without. I studiously avoided thinking about the dark magic I'd possessed just last week. Though I'd been able to use it to kill my opponents, it was just too evil to be trusted. Fortunately, it was strapped down deep inside me, no longer able to burst free. Which allowed me to use the new water magic I'd been gifted by some unknown god.

I could feel the new power in my chest, light and fresh and good. It connected to the water in the alley down below, making the liquid feel like it was part of me. As I sprinted away from it, my magic stayed connected, and I drew the water up from the alley. I could feel it rising through the air, an extension of myself.

When it was at my level, I glanced back just in time to see the shining silver liquid slap Lavender in the face. She shrieked and stopped dead in her tracks, rage lighting up her face as her hair dripped.

Oh, shit.

She was going to want revenge. She could probably throw a car at me.

Worth it.

I turned back around to sprint away, then stopped dead in my tracks.

Three demons stood in front of me.

Damn it.

There'd been rumors they would be thrown into the mix to make our job harder, and since the Protectorate pulled no punches, the demons wouldn't either. They had orders to kill, and they'd fulfill them with glee. If we couldn't survive their attacks as students—we were adults, after all—we wouldn't survive them as staff.

I eyed the three of them, grateful to see that they weren't huge, at least. No bigger than me, with wiry muscles underneath pale blue skin. Skin like that normally indicated ice powers, but I couldn't sense that magic on them. Instead, they wore black leather vests decorated with weapons. Knives, skinny swords, and throwing stars hung off the vests, glinting threateningly in the moonlight. Their short horns were sawed off, a demon affectation I'd never understood.

But it was their fangs that made me shiver. Long and dripping with saliva, the fangs made them look like barn animals from hell.

I mean, come on. That was so Old McDonald.

Normally, when faced with a demon, I'd reach into my handy bag of potions and hurl one at my enemy, but Jude had told me not to bring them to the race. I was supposed to be focusing on my new magic, and the potions were just a crutch.

But there was no water.

I'd used it up on Lavender.

I reached for the dagger strapped to my thigh. It was from my mother, a gift I rarely used. I raised it and aimed at the closest demon, hurling the steel. It spun, end over end, then thudded into the demon's chest.

He hissed in shock, his eyes widening.

"Come on, dude. I didn't exactly hide the thing," I muttered.

He'd had a second to dodge, but apparently his reflexes were slow. Fortunately, there was no need for guilt. His body might die, but he'd wake up in whatever underworld he'd come from, ready to go again. Demons weren't supposed to be on earth anyway, considering the havoc they wreaked. They were frequently hired by dark magic practitioners to do their dirty work, and I had a feeling that the Protectorate had found these guys somewhere that they shouldn't have been and offered them a second chance.

I could just imagine Jude making the offer: "Hunt our students during this race, and if you live, you're free."

But she'd known they wouldn't live. We might just be students, but we were skilled and deadly, and demons were obvious targets. I couldn't just leave them here, even if I could race past them. They could go on to do all kinds of terrible things.

Footsteps thudded behind me, and I didn't need to turn back to know that my competitors had jumped across the alley.

I sprinted forward, my gaze glued to the two demons who stood over the body of their fallen comrade, not sparing a glance for him as he bled out. Each drew a long sword that crackled with electric energy.

Ooh, those look fun.

I could just imagine adding one to my arsenal. As I sprinted, I drew a sword from the ether. It was a handy trick, storing weapons in the ether. Though the spell was expensive, it was worth it. The hilt of my sword felt comfortable in my hand as I neared my opponents.

Out of the corner of my eye, I spotted an icicle flying by. It glittered in the moonlight as it slammed into the chest of the demon on the right. The beast grimaced, then fell straight backward.

Well done, Lorence.

I was close enough to the third demon to smell the rank scent of him.

"Gah, you need a bath." I raised my steel, swiping out for his waist.

He sucked in, ducking back, and raised his electric sword. Blue light crackled around it, bright and fierce. Pretty, but deadly.

He swung, his movement fluid, and I ducked low, not daring to stop his blade with my own. If it really was electric, I didn't want to get a jolt up the arm.

The blade whizzed by over my head, so close that the crackle of electricity made my hair stand on end. My heart thudded as I moved, left, out of his range, then lunged forward with my sword.

The blade sank into his side, and he screeched, a high-pitched yowl that made my ears hurt. Behind him, my four competitors raced forward, taking the lead.

"I don't have time for you." I grunted as I pulled my sword free and dodged his second blow.

The hole in his side made him weak and slow, and I scooted out of the way quickly, narrowly avoiding an electric swipe to the arm. I lunged again, swinging my blade for his throat.

The steel connected with flesh, cutting deep. I ducked, trying to avoid the arterial blood flow. It was my *least* favorite part of a fight, and I avoided neck shots when possible, but I was in a hurry here.

The blood flew over my head, missing me.

Heck yeah!

Then a spray hit me right in the face, warm and disgusting.

Damn it.

I scowled and dragged my sleeve over my face as the demon fell. He crashed to the ground, his electric sword rolling to a stop at his side. I bent and grabbed it, then recovered my mother's dagger and shoved it in my thigh sheath. Quickly, I sprinted after my competitors.

They were a good twenty yards ahead of me, having joyfully left me behind to deal with the demons, and each was jockeying for the lead. Lavender hurled random street debris at her opponents, while Carl and Lorence threw their fire and ice, respectively. Angus threw blasts of electricity, but his aim was shit and he missed every time. He was fast, though, and he was ahead of the rest of them, sprinting ahead on swift legs until Lavender slammed a cinderblock into his foot.

As they neared the edge of their building, approaching another gap where an alley cut through, a horde of demons appeared, climbing up from the alley below.

There had to be a dozen of them, and holy crap, were they big.

I gripped my electric sword tightly, debating. I didn't really want to fight those guys. No doubt I'd end up with more demon blood on my face. I just needed a shortcut, or a way around, while I left my competitors to take them out.

Fair was fair, after all.

Hey! Down here!

The squeaky voice from below caught my attention. I hurried to a narrow gap between the buildings. It was only about three feet wide, a tiny alley that cut through two old brick structures that had to have been eighteenth-century tenements.

I peered down into the dark, catching sight of two gleaming eyes. There were two more sets off to the side.

"Romeo?" I whispered. "That you?"

The little raccoon scoffed. *Course it's me! How many alleyway experts do you know?*

Not that many, now that he mentioned it.

Come on! He waved his little paws, gesturing me down. *Shortcut here, no demons.*

Was I really going to trust him?

I looked back up at the fight that had broken out twenty yards ahead of me. The battle was fierce, and the blood was flying.

Yeah, I wanted no part of that. Anyway, I liked my T-shirt. The pink tie-dye looked cool with the rest of my black leather, and I didn't really want a bunch of demon blood on it. The stuff was a bitch to get out.

"Okay, I'm coming!" There was a rickety fire ladder to my left, and I hurried to it, then slipped down into the alley as quickly as I could without letting go of my new electric sword. The climb down was iffy, but no way would I leave my new blade behind. I couldn't just shove it in the ether because it didn't have a spell on it yet, so I had to hold on to it.

Hurry! Romeo said. *Poppy is hungry and Eloise wants to join the fight up there, so I don't have all day.*

I raced over to the raccoon, eyeing the possum and badger.

As usual, Poppy the possum wore a flower behind her ear and looked at me with just a slight tinge of judgement, while the badger shifted eagerly on her feet, ready to go to war.

Romeo, looking like a furry masked bandit, gestured with a little paw. *This way. Through here.*

He turned and sprinted down an even narrower alley, and I followed. Buildings had been built over the alley, hiding it from the sky. So that was why I hadn't seen it from up above.

"We must be going right under the fight," I said.

Yep! Romeo trundled along in front of me.

Eloise made a disgruntled noise from behind me, and I swore I heard her mutter, *Pity.*

"Did you just talk, Eloise?"

She didn't respond. Maybe I'd imagined it, but I didn't have time to dwell on it now. Instead, I sprinted through the darkened corridor.

"We're headed toward the castle, right?" I asked.

Yep. Just a shortcut.

"I can't believe I'm trusting a trash panda," I said.

Of course *you should trust me. I'm your divinely ordained sidekick. All Dragon Gods get one, and you were lucky enough to get me.*

He was right on that, at least. Bree had a trio of pug dogs, and Ana had a trio of cats. I had the Menacing Menagerie.

And I'll take trash panda as a compliment, thank you very much, Romeo continued. *Trash and pandas are both delightful.*

I grinned. "Of course it was a compliment."

The little raccoon liked trash so much that he rejected his standing invitation into the Protectorate kitchens in favor of rooting through the garbage for treasure, as he called it. Poppy and Eloise were always by his side, of course, and I suspected that it was actually Poppy who ran this show. Eloise was the muscle and Romeo the charm.

Almost there, Romeo muttered as he careened left, down another narrow tunnel.

Ancient Edinburgh was full of these creepy underground spaces, but if these critters could help me win this race, I'd take it. Romeo seemed to know all the ins and outs.

"Hey, Romeo, you know how to get into the castle?" I didn't know what to expect when we reached the final obstacle on this course, but I had to guess that breaking in was a requirement.

He glanced back over his shoulder. *The toilets. Duh.*

I grimaced. "Toilets?"

Yep. Ancient toilets. Just a straight drop through the castle walls. Like a little tunnel.

Holy fates, this raccoon was nuts.

There's a few of them, but the widest drop chute is the one to the left of the main gate, around the side and under the tall tower.

"Fantastic." He didn't seem to register the sarcasm in my tone.

Nearly there. Romeo hurried out into a wider alley, and I followed, Poppy and Eloise at my heels.

Here. Romeo stopped abruptly next to a big dumpster, pressing his hand to it.

"The dumpster?"

He glared at me, seeming to not even realize that he'd touched it and was now petting it lovingly. Eloise and Poppy sidled up to it as well.

No, silly. He pointed up. *The ladder.*

I looked up, spotting another fire ladder. This one, however, looked like it had been built two hundred years ago and then survived a whole lot of fires afterward. Barely survived.

"Um, Romeo, I don't think I can climb that. It's got pieces missing." I pointed to where the ladder had rusted through. "That thing is deadly."

Romeo looked at me with big, innocent eyes. *I didn't realize you were a wimp.*

I scowled at him, stifling a laugh at the subtle prodding.

You should do it, he continued. *Try to win the prize. It might be a lot of trash.*

Poppy and Eloise shifted excitedly.

"Doubtful." But I did need to find a way up onto the roof, and fast. The castle was on a higher elevation than the Grassmarket, so racing across the rooftops made sense. We needed to make it to the stairs that led the rest of the way up to the castle on the cliff.

"What are you doing on the ground, you idiot?" Lavender's voice echoed from above.

Damn it, she must have pulled into the lead.

Eloise stood up on her hind legs, growling.

"I knew you couldn't hack it." Lavender laughed.

Hot tar boiled in my chest, frustration following on its heels. Lavender was done fighting the demons, and she was getting a move on. No way I was going to let her beat me.

This had gone from *just stay alive and don't be an idiot* to *I will crush my enemies under my boot* in about two minutes flat.

"Fine." I looked at Romeo. "I'll haunt you if this ladder kills me."

He bowed. *I'd be honored.*

Another laugh bubbled in my throat as I stuck the hilt of the sword between my teeth and bit down. It was freaking hard to hold it like that, but I needed both hands to climb and I really didn't want to lose my new toy. I didn't dare stick it through my belt for fear that the electric blade would shock me.

I reached up and grabbed the rusty ladder, then began to climb.

Good luck! Romeo shouted from down below.

I was going to need it. The ladder was so rickety under my

hands that it could break any moment. As quickly as I could, I scaled upward. Near the top, the thing creaked and shifted. My heart jumped into my throat and my palms turned sweaty.

Oh fates.

I scrambled up faster, frantic to reach the top. I was nearly there when the ladder shrieked and groaned, the anchors in the wall breaking free of the stone. I clung to the metal as it bent away from the building, the movement torturous and slow. Finally, the top of the ladder touched the building on the other side of the alley, swinging me over the narrow street below.

My stomach lurched as my palms sweated and my feet dangled.

Never trust a trash panda.

CHAPTER TWO

Sweating, muscles aching, I slowly climbed onto the other side of the ladder so I was at least on top of it. As I made my way to the wall, the metal shifted, rusty flakes falling down like reddish-orange snow.

My heart thundered and my breath came short.

Thank fates I was near the top. I grabbed a windowsill and climbed on, then shimmied up. As soon as I flopped onto the rooftop, I let the sword fall from my mouth and rubbed my jaw. Damn, I was sore.

"Hurry!" Bree's voice flowed from the comms charm. "Lavender is getting ahead."

I scrambled to my feet, catching sight of Angus, Carl, and Lorence fighting another group of demons. Lavender had left them behind, and frankly, I didn't blame her. They weren't outnumbered, so they should be fine.

I turned to follow Lavender and made a running leap to get across the narrow alley. I pushed my muscles as hard as I could, ignoring the burn. She was nearly to the edge of the Grassmarket, at the section where this neighborhood butted up to the cliff upon which sat the castle. There were narrow stairs leading up

HUNT FOR MAGIC

to the front of the castle, and no way I could let her get there before me.

For some reason, she'd stopped right at the edge of the roofs and seemed to be staring at the flight of stairs that led upward.

Why the hell wasn't she racing forward? She was almost there.

A roar split the night, making the hair on my arms stand on end.

Holy fates, *that* had to be why she wasn't going forward.

Whatever was blocking her path sounded *big*. The Protectorate had to have used a spell to hide this from humans. We were in the supernatural neighborhood, but the castle was near the Royal Mile, where humans could go. And this monster had to be right next to it, from the sound of his roar.

I pushed myself harder, joining Lavender at the edge of the roof. I stared at the steep flight of stairs that led upward to the Royal Mile and the castle. It was bordered on one side by the building upon which we stood, and on the other side by the cliff upon which the castle sat. A huge monster loomed on the stairs, his body roughly human shaped and seeming to be made of stone. His eyes flared bright orange, like flames.

He raised a massive rock hand. Red glowed in his palm, like fire or molten lava.

"Oh fates. Duck!" I dived for the ground as the giant released the blast of fire.

Lavender followed, lunging to the ground alongside me. The flame plowed toward us, surging overhead. The heat was so close that it burned my forehead, and I buried my face in my arms. The creature roared again, the noise cutting through the thundering sound of my heart.

I raised my head to steal a peek, able to spot the top of the monster on the stairs. He raised his hand, which was beginning to glow a faint peach color.

17

"He's recharging." I scrambled to my feet and looked around for a plan.

Lavender joined me. "So, we're cooperating on this?"

I looked at her, incredulous. "I don't like you, Lavender. But I don't like *him* more."

"Fair enough." She turned back to the monster. "I tried to hit him with a rubbish bin earlier, but he was too fast."

So I needed to slow him down, then maybe she could nail him.

I spied a heavy rope that led up to a flag hanging from a pole overhead. It was a massive blue and white Scottish flag, and I really hoped people didn't get pissed when it hit the ground. I ran to it, then grabbed the rope and sliced through it with my electric sword.

"I'll yank him down, and you hit him with something heavy," I said.

Lavender rubbed her hands together. "I can do that."

I sidled up to the edge of the building. It was a fifteen-foot drop to the stairs below, which continued up higher to where the stone monster stood. "Distract him if you can."

"Got it." She raised her hands, and her magic fizzed on the air.

From the street below, a bicycle rose, then flew up the stairs, shooting toward the monster.

He dodged it, narrowly avoiding a strike to the middle. Lavender kept the bike floating, making it dart around his head like an annoying fly. He was fast enough to avoid it, but it distracted him.

Gripping my rope and sword, I jumped down onto the stairs below and raced upward. He was so distracted by the bike, which kept bopping him on the head, that he didn't even see me race around his legs with the rope.

Once I'd made a complete circle, I darted up and pulled

hard, my muscles straining. The rope tightened, yanking his feet out from under him. He crashed to the stairs below, landing hard.

He thrashed, trying to free himself, but he was awkward and slow. Lavender's magic surged hard, and a massive trash dumpster rose up from the street below and hurtled toward the stone monster. He tried to roll out of the way, but the stairs were too narrow.

It landed on him with a thud, and he lay still.

I grinned, then turned and sprinted up the stairs. I was heading into possible human territory, and had to keep a low profile. For this obstacle course, the Protectorate would have created barriers around the castle so the humans couldn't see us use magic, but I still needed to take a left at the top of the stairs and go about fifty yards up the Royal Mile in order to get to the castle. The street would be bustling with shops and bars, and chock full of humans.

Fortunately, with my black leather and pink T-shirt—and matching lipstick, of course—I would blend in nicely.

Except for the electric sword.

The thought almost stopped me in my tracks.

I didn't want to give up my new toy.

Crap.

I didn't slow my pace—Lavender was right behind me, after all—but I did look down at my beautiful new sword.

Double shit.

It definitely looked magical. No way to pass it off as a toy or prop, and I didn't need the attention. A frown tugged at the corner of my lips as I looked for a place to stash the sword. There were no good hiding places on this stairway, and odds on it being there when I came back to get it were slim.

But I didn't really have much choice, did I?

There was a little gap between two walls on my right, so I

shoved the sword inside and kept running. I could hear Lavender coming up from behind me and didn't pause.

When I reached the top, the Royal Mile looked normal. Loads of people bustled up and down the street, ducking into bars and late-night shops that sold all manner of trinkets and souvenirs.

It took everything I had to slow my frantic pace, but part of this job was stealth. A few people looked at me curiously, brows creased.

Oh crap, did I have blood on my face?

Quickly, I scrubbed at it again, hoping that I got the worst of the demon blood off. If I looked like the bad end of a horror film, the human cops might stop me. Then I'd definitely lose.

I was already doing so much better than I'd expected. I was neither dead nor totally embarrassed. I didn't want to ruin my streak.

As quickly as I could, I strode through the crowd, cutting up toward the castle. I got fewer weird looks, so I had to assume the demon blood was off my face.

A quick glance behind showed that Lavender was hot on my heels. Behind her, Carl, Lorence, and Angus appeared at the top of the steps.

Crap. I turned back and hurried faster, resisting a full-out run.

The castle loomed ahead, a monstrosity of stone and age that perched on a rock outcropping that sat in the middle of the city. From this side, the Royal Mile led up to it in a graceful slope. On the other three sides were cliffs, one of which led down into the Grassmarket.

The moon gleamed on the empty courtyard in front of the castle, and as soon as I stepped onto it, the sound of the bustling street below faded. I turned, and the scene of the street behind me was no longer clear. I was looking through a hazy barrier and couldn't really see what was going on out there. The street looked almost empty, in fact. Which meant they couldn't see me, probably.

As I'd thought, it'd been protected against human eyes so we could use magic.

Except there was no moat for me to manipulate, which would have been really danged handy.

Lavender stepped through the barrier a moment later, her gaze triumphant. She didn't even bother to look at me, just strode up to the massive wooden gate, her hands raised. Her magic swelled, and she directed her hands toward a huge iron cannon that sat in the courtyard.

Ah, crap.

The cannon lifted off the ground, wobbly at first. Then it picked up speed, shooting toward the castle gate.

Miserable witch. She was going to break the gate. It was probably ancient as hell and a historical artifact, and she was just going to smash it. The cannon slammed into the gate, shaking the wood.

I scowled, then turned, looking for another way in. Even if she smashed that thing right in front of me, I wouldn't follow her in on principle. But it wouldn't take her long to get through the gate with her method, so I'd need to be fast. I'd started this thing not wanting to die, and now I wanted more. I wanted to *win*. And maybe rub it in her face a tiny bit.

I searched the castle wall, hurrying around to the left. I was nearing the edge of the courtyard where it ended and the castle wall continued on, built right at the edge of the cliff. It looked like the cliff itself became the castle wall.

Please let there be some kind of entrance.

I could try to scale the wall, but it was pretty smooth. There weren't a lot of handholds. And there were no other entrances near where I was standing. I looked out over the castle wall that was built at the edge of the plummeting drop.

My gaze caught on a dark hole that was about level with my waist. It was at the base of the stone castle wall, right over the open drop down the cliff.

Understanding flared.

Romeo's toilet chute.

I eyed it, considering.

Oh fates, was I going to do this?

I looked around for any other option, but there was only smooth wall looming over top of me. My heart thundered as I approached the dark hole.

Just a peek. A sniff.

I mean, the thing clearly wasn't in operation anymore, right? I saw no *stuff* trailing down the cliff wall. In the medieval period, it would have poured right out and down the cliffside.

It was definitely big enough for me to fit through. And I wanted to win this.

Gingerly, I climbed onto the jagged cliff wall. I could just shimmy out there and climb up through the chute, as long as the interior walls had a few handholds.

Carefully, I climbed up to the chute's entrance—or exit, depending on your perspective. I shook my hand to ignite the magic in my lightstone ring and stuck my hand into the hole. I thrust my head in after, holding my breath, and looked upward.

The chute went all the way up, sandwiched inside the castle walls. It was narrow enough to prop myself up inside the walls, but not too narrow, and some of the sides had jagged rocks for handholds.

Tentatively, I sucked in a bit of air.

Stale, but not so bad. It definitely hadn't been used in centuries, and surely they'd tossed some water down here to clean it out, right?

I sure hoped so.

Because I *really* wanted to win.

I didn't waste any more time debating—just started shimmying up through the chute, propping myself up in the little tunnel and climbing.

Claustrophobia began to close in on me about halfway up when the chute narrowed some more, but I sucked in a shallow breath and kept going. I imagined winning.

Actually, I *had* to win.

Because if I lost and was found stuck in a medieval toilet, I would definitely fail at my goal of not dying of embarrassment.

In the distance, I could hear Lavender's cannon slamming against the castle gate. Good, she was still at it. I pushed myself faster, ascending like a chimney sweep. Frankly, I'd prefer that this *was* a chimney.

By the time I made it to the top, I was lightheaded from exertion and nerves. There was a wooden lid at the top, into which a hole had been cut. To illustrate the purpose of the little room, I had to assume.

I had a mental image of a big, pale butt sitting on the toilet seat over top of me and almost laughed. A gag was the only thing that stopped the noise, and in truth, it was easy to gag at the idea of that happening.

At the top, I pushed on the wooden board with the hole cut into it. The thing lifted easily, and I shimmied out into a small room built on the castle wall. The guards' toilet back in the old days, I had to assume.

No time to explore, though I did think it was pretty interesting.

Instead, I hurried out onto the rampart and searched for the flag. It was supposed to be on top of the tallest tower. When I didn't spot it, my heart fell briefly.

Then I heard the slam of Lavender's cannon as it finally

broke through the castle wall. She wasn't in yet, so the flag should still be here. No way Angus, Carl, or Lorence had beaten her.

What had Romeo said about a tower near the toilet?

I looked up, and realized that it loomed right behind me. I hadn't noticed it when I'd had eyes only for the toilet. But it was here, right next to me, reaching into the sky with a flag fluttering from the top.

Heck yeah.

I turned and began to scale the tower, hand over hand until I reached the top. It was one of those crenelated tops with a big platform in the middle. I was about to climb onto the flat surface when magic flared on the air, my only warning. I looked down just in time to see Lavender standing below me, her hands raised. I didn't have time to search for whatever was flying at my head—I just lunged onto the top of the tower, ducking.

A huge trash bin flew over my head.

That chick really had a thing for trash bins.

The bin slammed into the edge of the tower, trash flying everywhere. Romeo would have a field day. I scrambled to my feet, lunging toward the flagpole. Quickly, I grabbed my mother's knife from the sheath at my thigh and sliced through the rope. The flag fell, and I caught it.

A grin spread over my face.

Hell yeah.

I'd won.

Except, I'd also climbed up through a toilet. Gingerly, I lifted my hand to my face and sniffed.

"What are you doing?" Lavender's voice cracked through the air.

"Nothing." I jerked my hand down. I didn't *think* I smelled.

Oh man, it seemed like the possibility for embarrassment hadn't quite passed.

Lavender scowled at me. "How the hell did you get up here?"

"I have my ways." Toilets.

I brushed past her, our truce over the stone giant forgotten, and climbed back down the side of the tower, the flag tucked in my back pocket.

When I landed on the main rampart, Bree was waiting for me, her silver wings glinting. I strode toward her, keeping my voice low. "Do I smell?"

She frowned at me, then her brows rose. "Ah, right. *That's* how you got in. I wondered what that hole in the wall was." She leaned forward and sniffed. "No. You're fine. There was nothing in the chute, right?"

"Not after all these years, but you never know." I wanted to wash my hands right away.

"Did she help you?" Lavender demanded from behind. "Because that's not fair."

I turned and grinned at her. "Nope. Just yelled in my ear that I'm a moron."

Lavender shifted and smiled a bit. "Well, she's not wrong."

"Hey!" Bree snapped. "Only I get to call my sister a moron. Or Ana. Sisters' privilege."

My smile widened. "Aw, I love you, Bree."

"Back atcha."

"Well done!" Jude's voice carried across the ramparts, and I turned, catching sight of her approaching. Jude's stride was long and confident, her braids bouncing against her back and her starry blue eyes glowing against her dark skin. Angus, Carl, and Lorence trailed behind her, pulling up short when they stopped.

"Well, Rowan, it looks like you won." Jude smiled broadly. "Let's meet at the Whiskey and Warlock for a celebratory drink. And you can collect your prize."

❧

25

Twenty minutes later, after cleaning up in the pub bathroom and retouching my lipstick—Murderous Magenta, this time, which often suited my mood when I had to deal with Lavender —I joined everyone out in the little room that acted as our unofficial hangout.

I stepped into the small space, tugging at my black leather jacket as I surveyed the scene. Jude sat on a bench against the wall, while Bree and my classmates crowded around the table that was in front of her.

I swung by the shining wooden bar where Sophie stood drying a glass. Today, the bartender's shirt read "Nessie is My Other Ride."

She spotted me and grinned. "I've got just the thing for you tonight."

"Really?" I leaned on the bar and smiled.

"Yep. New beer in from Orkney called the Skull Splitter. Really rich, kinda fruity."

"Sounds great." I loved trying new beers. New anything, really. I'd been kidnapped while still a teenager, so I'd missed out on a lot. I was determined to make up for lost time.

While she fetched the beer, I replayed the race in my head, searching for any ways that I could have done it better. If I wanted to graduate and join the PITs, I needed to be perfect.

Sophie returned, popping the top on a dark bottle and handing it over. "Your sister already paid."

"Thanks." I took the beer and sipped as I turned. The cold, refreshing bubbles tickled my mouth, a reward for a job well done.

I joined my friends, squeezing into a chair next to Bree.

Jude leaned forward. "Well done, Rowan. You won."

I raised my beer and tilted my head toward her.

Jude reached her hand under the table and pulled out the

electric sword that I'd hidden back on the stairs during the race. My eyes widened.

"It was good you ditched it," Jude said. "You couldn't have carried it down the Royal Mile without being noticed. But given your performance today, I think you deserve to keep it. As your prize for winning."

I grinned widely. "Really?"

I *loved* this sword.

"Really. An electric sword was going to be the prize for the winner, but you jumped the gun and took it for yourself." She tilted her head. "I respect that. I respect even more that you let it go when you knew it wouldn't help you achieve your goals. Even though you loved it."

My cheeks heated at the praise, and Jude held the sword out to me.

"Thank you." I grabbed the hilt, my smile growing wider. It would do well in my arsenal. The prize. I looked at Bree. "Can you get your guy to enchant this so it's stored in the ether for me?" It was the best spell in the world, that ether storage spell for weapons. I loved being able to yank them out at any time and use them.

Bree nodded. "I'll call Franklin and ask him."

"You rock." I didn't know the mage she bought the spells from, but she seemed to trust him and that was good enough for me.

I looked back at Jude.

"Well done," she said. "I think you have a bright—" Her eyes widened on something behind my shoulder, and I turned.

Maximus stood in the doorway, his shoulders filling the space. The gladiator mage and my unofficial trainer looked as good as ever, of course. Like a freaking fallen angel. He was well over six feet tall and all rangy muscle, with dark hair and blue eyes. He'd earned those muscles in the real Colosseum thou-

27

sands of years ago, and I was grateful to the god Virtus who'd brought him forward into present day.

That didn't mean I knew how to act around him, though. The attraction was off the charts, and we'd shared one kiss a couple days ago that we'd studiously avoided talking about. We'd had one fight training session before he'd been called away by the Order of the Magica on an emergency, and the tension had been insane. We'd been in a room with other students and staff, though, so it hadn't been the time.

But all of that combined to make me awkward as hell, of course. It was my MO most of the time, anyway.

His brilliant blue eyes moved straight to mine, and it became even harder not to think of our kiss. My heart immediately began thundering, and a horde of butterflies started having a party in my middle. I swallowed hard, trying to look cool and unaffected. Now was not the time to remember our kiss from two days ago, but I couldn't help it.

I nodded briefly and moved my gaze away. The last thing I needed was for my future boss to see me making eyes at a hot dude when I was supposed to be focusing on my work.

Would my classmates tell him I'd climbed in a toilet? The errant thought slipped into my head.

Would he kiss me again, or was I now Toilet Girl?

I *had* won though.

Worth it.

Maximus strode toward our table.

Jude stood. "Is there a problem?"

He nodded sharply.

"We'll go to the round room," Jude said, referencing the war room where we often held most of the major discussions.

Maximus shook his head. "This will do fine, actually. The relevant parties are here."

His gaze moved to me, and I blinked.

I was a relevant party?

I had no idea what he meant, but I was suddenly dying of curiosity.

Jude sank down onto the bench. "What's going on?"

Maximus pulled up a chair and sat. "The Order of the Magica has a possible lead on the two witches who committed the murders last week. A seer gave us a tip."

My gaze sharpened on him, my interest piqued. Those damned witches had turned into giant killer birds. Every time they'd killed, the dark magic inside me had erupted. To say that I was invested in catching them was an understatement. I was connected to them, even though I didn't want to be, and I sure as heck wanted to stop them. We might have bound them from harming with their beaks or claws, but they could still use some nasty magic when they were in their human forms.

"Where are they?" Jude asked.

"We believe they may try to infiltrate the Intermagic Games."

I leaned forward. "That big race with a fabulous prize at the end?"

My gaze darted to Bree, and her eyes were as wide as mine felt. We might have spent most of our lives broke and on the run, but even *we'd* heard of the Intermagic Games. They were a big freaking deal. Apparently the competitions were dangerous and fantastic and weird. They were often like an obstacle course with clues, and occasionally spectators could watch parts of the competition.

"The same," Maximus said. "Every five years, the Intermagic Games hosts the competition for the students from some of the great magic academies. It's dangerous, but the prize is always highly coveted, so people compete."

"We've never sent competitors," Jude said. "It's beneath our mission to compete in a game."

"I know." Maximus nodded. "But that's why we think you can

help us. We suspect that the witches won't compete formally—they don't have an invitation—but they'll try to infiltrate the games to steal the prize at the end. We want to enter the games and try to catch them."

"Why don't you just tell the Intermagic Games Council?" Lavender asked. "They'll cancel the games, and the witches won't get the prize."

"They won't cancel the games—they're too profitable. And we hold no jurisdiction there, so we can't force them. We're not sure we want to, anyway. This is a good opportunity to try to catch the witches, since we know where they will be. Even though this makes the games more dangerous, the contestants are aware that the race is deadly. They know the risks," Maximus said.

He was right. It was famously deadly, actually. Years ago—probably at the last games, since they ran every five years—two of the contestants had died in a giant snake pit. I shuddered at the thought.

"We want to send a team to the games," Maximus said. "That way, we can try to catch the witches. At the very least, we can try to beat them to the prize."

"I presume that's where we come in?" Jude asked.

Maximus nodded. "We've bought a spot for one team to enter." A grim smile stretched across his face. "The Intermagic Games Council is easily bought."

They must be, if they'd allow the games to go on despite the fact that evil witches were infiltrating.

Maximus continued. "Four teams of two compete in the games. We can send one team." His gaze moved to me. "I'd like Rowan to compete as my partner. They don't need to know that I'm not officially a student at the Academy. As long as we enter under your banner, we're fine."

My heart thundered. I liked the idea of being invited. I was also scared out of my wits. The snake pit, after all.

"If you've already bought a spot to compete, then the Intermagic Games Council is expecting our Academy to enter. You've already signed us up."

Maximus nodded. "The games start tomorrow. We didn't have much time. And I suspected that you would agree. This is too big of an opportunity to stop evil."

Jude frowned, but she nodded. "You're right. I want in. These witches are immensely dangerous to the well-being of the world, and we won't sit back if this is a chance to catch them. But I won't command Rowan to go." She turned to me. "Today you proved that you're the most qualified. But I leave it up to you if you want to be the Undercover Protectorate's champion at the games."

My eyes widened.

Champion? At the Intermagic Games?

Holy fates, that was a big deal. It even sounded cool.

More importantly—*much* more importantly—it was an opportunity to catch the witches. I had to take it. I was about to nod when I remembered what he said about the prize. "What's the prize?"

"This year, it's a Truth Teller," Maximus said.

A low gasp sounded through the group. A Truth Teller was a super-rare magical object. So rare that I'd never seen one. Probably no one at the table had seen one. They were almost mythical in their ability to tell you anything you wanted to know. Unlike a seer, who often had blind spots or could occasionally be downright wrong, the Truth Teller knew all.

It would be so valuable to the Protectorate. We'd be so much more effective at stopping bad guys and protecting the innocent. I wanted to win that for our side. We could catch the witches *and* take home the prize.

A selfish part of me piped up, deep inside. With a Truth Teller, I could find out what kind of Dragon God I was. I could figure out how to get rid of the dark magic inside of me. Forever.

"I'll compete if the Protectorate gets to keep the Truth Teller," I said. "If our team wins, that is."

Jude gave me an appraising look. "Quick thinking. Having a Truth Teller would be a huge boon for the Protectorate. It could help us with our cases. We could save countless lives with it."

We would help no matter what—I knew the Protectorate well enough to know that. But why not try for more?

And I suddenly wanted to win this thing. Somehow, I'd gone from having a goal of just staying alive in this smaller race to wanting to win an enormous, potentially fatal international competition hosted by the biggest magical government of them all. But I could really help the Protectorate by doing this.

Maximus frowned, then nodded. "I can arrange that."

"Perfect." I grinned. "Looks like things are about to get deadly."

CHAPTER THREE

The next evening, I waited outside of the Théâtre Rouge with Maximus. The ornate old theatre was a landmark in Paris, and the introductory part of the competition was supposed to take place here in front of an audience. The idea made me slightly nauseous. Traditionally, aspects of the competition were turned into a spectator sport, so the theatre made sense. I just wasn't a theatre kind of girl. At least, not the kind who wanted to be on the stage.

I eyed Maximus, who stood next to me. After drinks at the Whiskey and Warlock last night, he'd headed off immediately.

Which was fine. Really.

At least, that's what I was telling myself.

I'd also told myself that we wouldn't kiss again. That I was going to focus on my magic. Everything in my life was so chaotic —dark magic inside me, new magic I needed to learn to control, coursework at the Academy—that I didn't have time for a relationship.

Especially not with my trainer.

But as I stood next to him on the darkened street in Paris, the old street lamps glowing golden around us and the Eiffel Tower spearing the sky, it was hard to remember that.

Because damn, did he look good.

We'd been told to dress nicely for the introductory event—it was a spectator sport, after all, and we were the entertainment—and Maximus had listened. In his own way, at least. They certainly weren't formal clothes. He was ready to fight at the drop of a hat. But he wore all black, close fitting and perfectly tailored clothes that showed off his height and strength to perfection.

Jude had rejected my plans for a dress, saying that it was possible the competition would start immediately after the introductory show. I hadn't worn a dress in so many years that I was actually kind of excited about the possibility, but I was no dummy. I didn't want to be fighting for my life in a skirt and heels. Hard to run in stilettos, no matter how cool they looked. Not to mention that kicking in demon teeth was easier in boots.

So I'd settled for a pair of skinny black jeans—no holes!—and a sleek, short leather jacket that matched. Of course I wore pink lipstick—Magenta Magic, this time. But instead of my usual pink shirt, I'd chosen a slinky gold top that glittered.

A small leather bag hung crosswise over my back, stuffed full of potion bombs of all varieties. Gold hoops in my ears would have looked cool as hell, but again, impractical. A demon could yank one right out, and hell no to that. Gold studs instead, and fake, since I was basically broke. The Academy gave me a small stipend, but I was saving up just in case things went to hell here and I needed to make a life on my own outside.

That would mean leaving my sisters, though, and the idea made something tear inside me.

"Do you think this will start soon?" I asked, trying to distract myself from the horrible idea. That wouldn't happen. I wouldn't let it. I'd finally found them after so many years away, and nothing would make me let them go. I'd do whatever it took to win this thing, since it put me one step closer to becoming an official member of the Protectorate. Becoming an official member meant staying with my sisters. Forever.

Maximus looked at his watch and nodded. "The coordinator should be here any minute."

I shifted from foot to foot on the cobblestones, grateful I wasn't wearing heels. Honestly, as much as I liked the look of them, I'd probably fall on my ass.

Jude had explained that we were to meet a coordinator outside the back of the Théâtre Rouge. The front was bustling with supernaturals headed inside, ready for the show to start. The back was much quieter, a little street with old lamps shining golden light on the cobblestones. There were no other competitors here, and I wondered if they were inside. They'd had more time to prepare for this, after all.

The back door of the theatre opened, and a pale face peeked out. Small eyes and a pointed nose gave the figure a mousey appearance, but the brilliant golden hair and matching suit made him look like a cosmopolitan mouse, at least.

"Rowan Blackwood? Maximus Valerius?"

I stepped forward. "Yes."

He scowled and gestured us forward. "Come, come, it's about to start."

I shared a glance with Maximus, then hurried up the stairs.

The man was a good head shorter than me and skinny as a lizard. He held open the door, still gesturing and vibrating with nervous energy. I didn't point out that we weren't late, even though he was acting like it. Whoever he was, this was clearly a big night for him.

"All the other contestants are here. The stage is set. The

show is about to go on!" His bright eyes were as gold as his hair, and I wondered what species he was. In the darkness at the back of the theatre, I could hardly see anything.

"Come, come." He led us down the darkened hall toward the low rumbling of a crowd. I could just make out the sound of an announcer's voice, the rich tones booming through a sound system up ahead.

Honestly, it felt like we were walking toward a circus.

I leaned into Maximus. "This is much more of a show than I was expecting."

"I've never seen it." He frowned. "But I think we're going to be monkeys on display."

Monkeys on display? That had to be some old Roman expression.

Certain parts of the competition might have spectators watching, but there shouldn't be many of those. I'd have to keep my dark magic under wraps during those bits, though. And I'd successfully locked it down tight, I reminded myself.

The golden lizard man—who hadn't bothered to introduce himself, I realized—led us out onto the edge of a huge stage.

Bright golden light pooled on the wood floorboards, illuminating a skinny man dressed all in black. His top hat glittered with gems, the only color on his otherwise austere figure. His slick black hair flowed down his back, and he looked exactly like a snake oil salesman, as far as I was concerned. He even had a twirly villain mustache.

I glanced at the golden lizard man who was staring at the snake oil salesman with rapt attention. His gaze gleamed. "Isn't he fabulous?"

I blinked. "Um, yes?"

A snicker from my left caught my ear, and I glanced over, catching sight of a tall woman with white hair and white eyes. Despite the hair color, she looked young. No older than me, but a good six inches taller. She had an identical twin, and the magic that rolled off of them smelled strongly of sandalwood and dusty old stone.

Were they competitors?

White-eyes glanced at me, then narrowed her gaze.

I just grinned widely at her.

Yep, she was probably the competition, and I was going to crush her.

"It's time, ladies and gentlemen!" The snake oil salesman's voice boomed louder. "Time to meet our contestants! Time for the magic and mayhem to start, for the games to begin!"

My attention snapped back to the show, and I turned to look. From the other side of the stage, two other pairs of contestants walked out. Two fae—a man and a woman—their glittery wings held aloft. Fae didn't always keep their wings out, but here, it was part of the show. They were both slender and dark-skinned, their wings a brilliant blue that glittered underneath the bright stage lights. They, too, were dressed for battle—but nicely. Dark jeans were offset by flashy colored shirts, and magic sparkled around each of their hands.

The other pair was massive. Both men—one older and one younger—were nearly as big as Maximus. They had broad faces and scowls that could strip paint. From the earthy smell of their magic, they were both some kind of shifter. Their magic rolled across the stage, powerful and dangerous. An image of a wolf flickered over their forms. The beast snarled, white fangs gleaming.

I shivered. I'd never seen shifter magic like that. It was like a message—*I'm dangerous as hell and I'm here to tear your throat out.*

My skin crawled. All of them would be out to kill me.

Sure, Lavender wanted to throw heavy objects at my head and I jokingly called her my archnemesis, but we were still on the same team. Our angst was more competitive. This was deadly. These people were my enemies, and they'd strike to kill.

I glanced up at Maximus, whose brow was set in a serious line as he keenly observed our competitors. He was probably thinking the same thing, and I had a sudden flash of realization that this was what he would have looked like back in the day, when he'd been standing outside the gladiator ring.

I leaned into him. "Bring back memories?"

He nodded sharply. "And not good ones." He tilted his head toward the wolves. "They've killed before. Many times. They want to kill again."

"How can you tell?"

"It's written all over their faces." His frown deepened. "If there's anything I've learned, it's how to spot a killer."

He'd had enough practice, at least, with over a thousand matches in the Colosseum in Rome. For what felt like the tenth time, I was grateful he'd proven himself in the fights and the slave revolution that followed. If he hadn't done that, the Roman god Virtus never would have brought him forward in time and he'd still be stuck there, fighting to the death.

"Go! Go!" The hissing whisper broke through my thoughts. Then a hand shoved at my back, and I stumbled out onto the stage.

The lights blinded me, and I squinted, frozen to the spot. My heart seized and my muscles turned to stone.

Oh, hell.

Apparently, I had stage fright. Fan-freaking-tastic.

I hadn't expected this.

Maximus's large form appeared next to me, solid and real in the sea of lights. I reached for his hand and gripped it. He squeezed back, tethering me to the earth. I sucked in a deep breath and dragged myself back from the stupid fear.

Because it was stupid. I'd faced down truly deadly situations. This was nothing.

Not to mention, it would become *truly* deadly soon enough.

Together, we walked out onto the stage, joining the others. I could feel the stares of the crowd prickling across my skin, though I couldn't see them. There had to be thousands, though. The theatre was huge.

"In a competition most dangerous and strange, our four teams will compete to find the Truth Teller!"

I focused on the snake oil salesman's voice. I needed to hear this stuff. I *needed* to be ready.

"From all over the globe, they have come," he boomed. "Our competitors will risk life and limb during a challenge most surreal. Monsters and mayhem will collide in the race of a life-time. Not all will survive."

My ears perked up at that. *Not all will survive?* That sounded pretty damned certain. This was supposed to *maybe* be a death match. Not certainly.

The snake oil salesman turned to the fae. "From the Fae Academy of Lythosos, we have Jabari and Imani."

The two fae stepped forward, their smiles blinding as their wings glittered a vibrant sapphire. They threw up their hands, and shimmering blue magic burst forth. Dozens of birds appeared in the brilliant clouds, darting through the air, beaks sharp and eyes bright.

I'd bet good money that those birds would peck my eyes out in a heartbeat. More than likely, they were a weapon.

The snake oil salesman gestured to the wolves next. "And from the Wolf Preparatory Academy at Glencarrough, we have Fergus and Ewan Boswell."

The wolves' magic surged, smelling so strongly of wet dog that I held my breath. A second later, they shifted into huge wolves, their coats gleaming and bright. They sprinted toward the edge of the stage, then leaped up onto a hanging platform and then jumped onto another. They ran so fast and jumped so high that even I was impressed, and I'd seen some mega badass shifters before.

It was almost like they were dogs doing tricks, but they were so powerful and fast that it was actually a bit terrifying.

The snake oil salesman turned to the pale white women who stood next to us. By far, they were the creepiest of the lot. "Our third competitors come from the Illusionist School of St. Petersburg! Natalia and Olga Ivanov!"

They stepped forward, their movements so graceful that they almost looked like they were floating. When they raised their hands, I had a horrible, sinking suspicion that they were also about to perform some cool trick with their magic.

Which meant that Maximus and I would have to do the same.

Except there was no water around here for me to control.

And my only other power was unleashing the darkness inside me and obliterating my foes. Which was *not* an option.

As the illusionists created a fantastical light show with prancing unicorns—over the top, if you asked me—I looked at Maximus, my eyes wide.

He caught my gaze and nodded, then murmured, "I'll conjure, you control."

Wait, what?

Then the announcer was shouting our names. My heart thundered so loudly that I almost couldn't hear him announce the Protectorate Academy's name. Oh fates, I couldn't embarrass them by just *standing* still like a dummy.

Then Maximus's magic flared, the scent of cedar and the taste of fine whiskey tethering me to the ground. In front of him, water appeared out of thin air.

I caught on immediately, thank fates, dragging my magic up

from inside my soul and forcing it outward. Fates, this was difficult. I'd never used it so quickly, but I had to. If I didn't get my act together—and fast—we'd be standing in a giant puddle on the national stage, looking like we'd wet ourselves.

The Toilet Girl who'd wet herself.

I couldn't go down in history as *that*.

So I gave it my all, forcing the water upward, driving it into the air in a powerful stream. Sweat dripped down my back as I worked, straining. Maximus conjured more and more, and I gathered it up with my magic, forcing it to shoot around the room like a giant snake made of clear water.

I'd never done anything so intricate with my magic—I was more a smash-and-slam kinda girl—but we needed finesse for this. I had to live up to the unicorn light show. As I made the water zip around the room, I became more competent. I felt like there was a voice in my head, telling me what to do.

Was it the mysterious god who had given me this magic?

Most likely. That was how Dragon God powers worked, after all.

The idea that a god might be watching me—that one was helping me—made me shiver. But I never let up on the water. It was flowing in graceful swirls, dancing over the audience and never once dripping onto them. I created artwork in the air, dancing mermaids who looked a little weird but were recognizable, at least.

My muscles trembled with strain, and sweat dotted my skin. Damn, this was difficult.

As my grand finale, I spelled out *Intermagic Games*.

Then, with horror, I realized I had nowhere to put the water. It was too much to send down a nearby toilet. Frantic, I glanced around, looking for somewhere to dump hundreds of gallons. Not on the crowd. Fates knew we'd be the least popular team if I did that.

"To the right," Maximus whispered.

I looked right, catching sight of the Menacing Menagerie, sitting in front of a large glass window that they had pushed open. All three of them were gesturing wildly to me.

My heroes.

I shot the water toward the window, and it zipped through, a clear snake that flowed out into the night air. If I focused hard enough, I could feel a large body of water nearby. The Seine. It had to be. I sent the water toward the large river that cut through the city and dumped it in, praying that I had good aim.

While I took care of that, the crowd's applause died down and the show started up again. I winked at the Menacing Menagerie, then turned back to the announcer, still vibrating from the tension.

"They'll set off on their adventure soon, going to lands uncharted," he boomed. "They'll follow clue after clue, and only the smartest and strongest will survive."

There he went again, assuming some of us would bite it.

Well, it wouldn't be us.

He spun to face the contestants. "Your goal on this first mission will be to find the ghost in the attic. He will give you your first clue."

Ghost in the attic? What the heck did that mean? I didn't have a chance to ask before he was spinning back to the audience.

"And for our viewing pleasure this year, we have something fantastic in store! Our technomages have been hard at work these last five years, working on an advancement that will allow us to follow every single second of the adventure."

My attention snapped toward him. *Every single second?*

The announcer waved his hands, and tiny white lights zipped out from backstage, swirling around our heads like annoying gnats. "These wisps will follow our champions, providing us with a spectacular view throughout the entirety of the journey!"

He gestured to the wall behind us, and I turned, dread spreading through me like inky black fog.

Behind us, an image was projected at the back of the stage. It was all of us, standing beneath the bright lights.

Oh, crap.

This wasn't good.

I'd been prepared to be on display *some* of the time. In years past, some of the competition was staged in arenas and covered by reporters. It would have been easier to hide that way.

This was another matter altogether. They would watch us every second.

Though the image that they displayed was a bit hazy and watery, there was no hiding the fact that it was us. If my magic went haywire, they'd all see it. And this was hosted by the Order of the Magica, the ones with the power to toss me in a cell in the Prison for Magical Miscreants.

I sucked in a deep breath.

Chill.

I'd gotten the dark magic under control. I'd known that when I'd chosen to do this. It was still within me, but it wasn't bursting out anymore. I could keep it that way. I would be okay.

And if new magic shot to the surface, more gifts from the gods, I'd just have to hope that none of it was creepy or super dangerous. With my luck, they'd give me some kind of horrible death power. But I'd cross that bridge when I came to it.

The announcer was finishing his spiel, going on and on about the dangers and wonders to come. Tension vibrated across my skin as I waited.

Let's just get started already!

I wanted to shout the words, but I bit them back. Crazy

outbursts would not be good, no matter how anxious I was to get the hell out of here.

Then my wish was granted.

Smoke and lights exploded around me, glittery gray that blinded me. I lunged for Maximus, grabbing onto him just as the ether sucked us in, throwing us across space and spinning us toward the danger that the announcer had promised.

CHAPTER FOUR

The ether spat us out into the cold darkness. I stumbled, almost going to my knees on the soggy ground.

Yep, glad I wasn't wearing heels.

In the distance, a wolf howled.

I shook my hair back from my face and spun around, taking in our location.

Maximus and I stood alone on a dark and lonely moor. The hills rose and fell in the distance, each of them topped with a cluster of granite stones. Moonlight shined into the shallow valleys, gleaming off rivers that cut between the hills. Wind whipped my hair back from my face, and I felt like a heroine from some gothic novel, out to wander the misty moors.

I shook my head.

No time for crazy fantasies. Because we were currently *in* a crazy fantasy. On the hill that had been directly behind us, a creepy old mansion rose tall. Lights glowed from within the house, but the whole thing was in incredible disrepair. Shutters hung loose, and the door was literally chained shut. We were over a hundred yards away, and I could still see the chain—that was how freaking big it was.

"That's a haunted house if I've ever seen one," I muttered.

Maximus chuckled low in his throat as he scanned our surroundings. "I don't see our competitors."

"One of them is howling."

"I don't think that's a wolf. It's slightly different. A hound of some sort."

A memory flashed. "*The Hound of the Baskervilles*?"

"What's that?"

I'd been reading a lot in my spare time, since I recently realized how much I missed books during my captivity. "A spectral hound that haunts Dartmoor. The fictional creation of Sir Arthur Conan Doyle. Sherlock Holmes is the hero."

"It doesn't sound so fictional now."

"No." And I wouldn't be surprised if I found Rochester's crazy wife in the attic of that house, though Eyre had taken place on a different misty moor.

"If we're looking for the ghost in the attic, I bet that's the place." I pointed toward the house that sat on the hill opposite ours. A shallow valley stretched between us and our target.

Maximus nodded.

The hound bayed again, and the hairs on my arms stood up. "He's getting closer."

"Let's move."

We cut across the soggy ground, the chill wind biting through my jacket. As I jogged down the hill, heading toward the house, pale white lights appeared, flitting around my head.

I smacked at them, then glanced at Maximus. "This is going to be annoying."

He nodded, expression grim.

I'd have to be careful what I said around the white wisps. They continued to flit, but I did my best to ignore them, picking up my pace as the sound of the hound grew nearer.

"It's stalking us," Maximus said.

I looked around, but saw no hound. No sign of life either. Just a massive circle of low stones on the hill beside us. They formed a low, broken-down wall that surrounded an area the size of a football field. We cut straight through, passing by smaller circles made of more stones. This place was ancient—I could feel it in my bones, but I had no idea what it was.

We reached the low valley and jogged up the hill toward the house. It loomed overhead, a specter in and of itself. The ghost of a house that had once sat here. Once normal, it was now a creepy shadow of itself. The air began to prickle.

"Feel that?" I asked.

Maximus nodded. "Protection charm. Once we pass the barrier, we won't be able to transport."

A dozen yards later, the protection charm seemed to pop as we crossed over it. If we wanted to make a run for it later, we'd need to reach this point and then go a bit farther.

We arrived at the front lawn—or what passed for it—and had to pick our way through a massive bed of pale green pumpkins. A few orange ones were scattered amongst the lot, but most were a ghostly gray green. The fat vines twisted like snakes along the grass, and I dodged them, jumping over the pumpkins. Mist floated over the ground, making it hard to see, but I made it to the front step of the house without tripping and falling on my face, thank fates.

The door really was chained shut, the huge iron links criss-crossing over the old wooden door. A dark window sat next to it, and I crept up to it.

Behind us, the hound howled louder. Closer now.

My heart thundered. I looked back, but saw only mist. It had risen up off the ground and now hid the other hills. I shivered and turned back to the window, peering inside.

It was dark and empty. "I can't see anything."

Maximus appeared close behind me, looking in. His heat seeped through the back of my jacket, and I nearly sighed.

The hound howled, louder, and I snapped back to attention.

"There's something in there." Maximus leaned closer, his front pressing to my back.

To our left, the door creaked open. We jumped and spun to face it.

A witch glared out, her face haggard and a wart on her nose. Her dress was shapeless and black, and she wore a ratty, pointed hat.

Holy crap. I'd seen a lot of witches in my day, and *none* had looked like this.

She looked like a freaking cartoon.

But mean.

She hissed, revealing fangs. "What are you doing there, trespassing on my land?"

Ice shivered down my spine. This was one woman you did not want to mess with.

"We're here to see the ghost in the attic." Maximus's voice revealed no fear.

Her face contorted, an expression of rage and pure evil. "Goooo!"

She shouted the word so loudly that I went deaf, my ears ringing. Her bellow whooshed over me, shaking the porch upon which I stood. Fire gleamed in her eyes, and her magic swelled.

"Time to go." I was too deaf to hear my words, but Maximus got the point.

We darted off the porch, running like our lives depended on it. The mist swallowed us up, and I grabbed his hand, pulling him left. We couldn't just abandon the house. We needed to get into that attic. But going in through the front door was *not* an option.

I tugged him left, heading around the house to the side.

The hound bayed again, the sound tinny through my returning hearing, and I could tell that it was close. Too close.

We needed to find a way in before the hound reached us.

I pressed my back against the side wall of the house, and Maximus joined me.

He leaned close and whispered against my ear. "I saw a low window a dozen feet ahead. Into a basement, maybe."

I shivered at the feel of his breath against my ear. No. Now was not the time. Between the deadly dog and the zipping white wisps that followed our every moment, this was decidedly the *worst* time to be thinking about Maximus's mouth.

I nodded and moved, hurrying along the edge of the house on silent feet.

Just as Maximus had said, there was a window near the ground. Broken.

I knelt and inspected the debris, spotting a paw print. I looked up. "The wolf brothers were here."

"They're already inside." A grim expression crossed Maximus's face. "Let's go."

The hound howled again, this time so close that I swore I could smell its deadly breath.

I scrambled through the broken window, trying to avoid the glass. Maximus followed. I looked back out the window just in time to see the dog's massive head, his jaws snapping at us.

I lurched backward, but the dog didn't follow. He was too big.

Shaking and sweaty, I turned from it to face the damp, dark basement. The room was large and the ceiling low, and the scent of dirt was strong down here. Though the wisps provided a tiny bit of light, it was still too dark to see much.

The sound of the dog's growl was punctuated by a thumping noise that came from about twenty feet away, and I jumped.

My heart thundered, and I shook my lightstone ring. A golden glow flared, illuminating a coffin on a low table.

"What the heck?" I murmured.

It thumped again, like there was someone inside.

"It's locked." Maximus pointed to a heavy old padlock that shut the coffin up tight.

I approached, my footsteps quiet. The lock was so ancient that it was rusted. A skeleton key would open it. "It's been locked for years."

It thumped again, so hard that the coffin bounced. Whoever was inside *heard* us. But why was it locked? Were they dangerous?

The wolf shifters had just ignored the coffin, heading on.

If we ignored it, too, we'd maintain the element of surprise. If we released whatever was inside, it could be dangerous. It could be loud.

I *really* didn't want to alert the witch.

But I also really didn't want to leave someone locked up. He —or she—might be evil. But maybe not.

I looked at Maximus. "I think we should let it out."

He nodded, frowning. "It's dangerous. But we have no other choice."

"Exactly." I liked that he was on my side in this. I touched the lock. "How are we going to get this open?"

Maximus reached out and nudged my hand aside, then grabbed the lock and yanked. The metal latches tore away from the coffin.

The lid burst open, and a vampire popped up, sitting upright, his face pale and his dark eyes wide.

I jumped, heart pounding, and drew a sword from the ether.

The vampire turned to us. He wore a long black cloak with a high collar. His dark hair was slicked back from his head, and his fangs were long and white. I blinked.

He looked exactly like a Hollywood version of a vampire.

His gaze met mine, and he spoke, his Transylvanian accent thick. "I vant to suck your blood."

My jaw almost dropped. "Are you serious?"

He blinked. "You are not scared?"

"Of your breath, maybe." But not of him. Not anymore. I could read danger. And it wasn't this guy. I turned to Maximus. "Breath mint?"

Maximus looked at me, slightly startled. Then a smile quirked at the edge of his mouth, and he conjured a breath mint and handed it to me. I passed it over to the vampire.

He looked down at it, confused.

"Put it in your mouth."

He took it and popped it into his mouth, his fangs gleaming. Then his eyes brightened. "Oh, that's quite nice."

"I thought you might like that." And this was officially super surreal.

"What are you doing here?" Maximus asked. "Did the witch capture you?"

"Years ago, yes. More than a century. We're mortal enemies." He scowled, sucking furiously at the mint. "I am Dracula."

My brows rose. "*The* Dracula?"

"There are others?"

Now was not the time to mention the thousands who dressed up at Halloween. Or the movies. Better for him to figure it out on his own. "Do you know anything about a ghost in the attic?"

He shook his head. "Nothing. But I do know that you should not go farther into this house."

I frowned. "We have to."

"Then it was very nice to make your acquaintance, but I fear it will not be a long-lasting friendship. For you shall be dead soon."

"Fantastic." I smiled at him. "Any tips other than that?"

"Avoid the mummy in the kitchen."

"Mummy?" Maximus asked. "Someone's mother is there?"

I glanced at him, a grin on my face. Most times, it was easy to forget that he was from the past. He had a grasp on almost every aspect of modern life. But apparently not mummies.

"No, not someone's mother," I said. "A mummy is a dead body that has been dried out and wrapped up in cloth. It's a burial ritual. Also a common feature in haunted houses." Which this one was really turning out to be. First a witch, then Dracula, and finally a mummy, if we were unlucky enough to run into him.

Speaking of, the wolves were already ahead of us, and if this was all the advice Dracula had, we needed to get a move on.

"Well, we'll be on our way," I said.

"Yes, yes. Me too." The vampire nodded, his expression serious. Then a poof of magic burst from him, a pale light that swallowed his form. A moment later, a small bat appeared, fluttering in midair. The little beast gave a fangy smile, then darted away, flying out the window.

I shook my head, looking at Maximus. "This is freaking surreal."

"How so? They're just monsters."

I smiled. "I'll show you some old movies sometime, just so you can get a feel for how weird this crowd is."

Only once I'd said it did I realize that it kind of sounded like a date. That was exactly what a date was, in fact. Watching old movies. Together. Alone.

A slow, sexy smile tugged at the corner of his mouth. "I'd like that."

I nodded, suddenly feeling awkward. Not only were the wisps following us, blasting this exchange across the world for viewers to enjoy, but I wasn't willing to live up to my promise.

I didn't want a relationship. Not even a friends-with-benefits one. Not when my life was such a mess. So I really needed to not make date suggestions like that. It could go nowhere good.

I turned, looking for an exit. "Let's go."

It didn't take long to find a rickety set of stairs heading upward. As we climbed, I murmured, "This has been okay so far. Mean dog, scary witch, and a funny vampire. Not so bad, really."

"That's what I said when they tossed me in the gladiator ring." Maximus's voice was serious. "I was wrong."

I glanced back at him. "Famous last words, then?"

"Perhaps."

He was probably right. I turned back and continued climbing, my footsteps silent. The door at the top was made of old, scratched wood. I pushed it open, and it creaked, shrieking like a banshee. I stiffened, then slipped through the narrow opening.

Straight into a graveyard.

I stopped, my brows flying upward. "What the heck?"

Those had definitely been famous last words, because the place reeked of danger.

Maximus shoved me lightly, and I stepped forward, giving him room to move through the door. My foot landed on something squishy, and I looked down to see a decayed gravesite flower, crushed against the wooden floor.

Wooden floor?

So we were still in the house?

I looked around, taking in the massive graveyard. It was the size of a football field, at least. Gray headstones stuck up from the ground, many of them at crazy angles. Mist hovered over the ground, sneaking between the stones. Here and there, transparent white ghosts floated. They were amorphous, looking a bit like the kinds of ghosts that were made from sheets at Halloween. Usually, ghosts looked like shadowy versions of their former selves.

Not these ghosts. They looked tattered and worn, like they were barely hanging on to the world.

And somewhere amongst all this, that creepy witch was lurking. I stepped closer to Maximus, studying our surroundings. "I think we're still inside the house. Though it's a lot bigger than I realized."

He pointed to the right. "There's a window, just there."

I squinted toward it, catching sight of a glass pane that floated in midair. I couldn't see the wall itself, but the graveyard ended right before the window.

"This really is surreal." That snake oil announcer hadn't been lying.

The cold mist that hovered over the ground was sneaking into my boots, making my feet feel unnaturally cold. Something about it reminded me of death, and I knew instinctually that I didn't want to be standing in it for long.

"We need to find some stairs." I started forward on quiet feet, avoiding the headstones as I kept my eyes on the ghosts.

There was no moon overhead since we were inside, but I couldn't see a ceiling. An eerie glow hung in the air, illuminating the graveyard enough that I didn't fall on my face.

Lit jack-o'-lanterns sat on some of the graves, but they were tiny and weird-shaped. Carved from turnips, I realized. There were a few small green pumpkins as well, and the effect was like some horrible Halloween farce.

Then I spotted Romeo, sitting with his back to one of the gravestones and snacking on one of the lanterns. Poppy and Eloise sat next to him, each of them clutching a turnip carved with a face.

Romeo's gaze darted up to meet mine, and he grinned broadly, holding out the turnip. *You should try one. The candle gives it such a nice toasty flavor.*

"Do those count as trash?" I asked, not even bothering to ask how he'd gotten here. It seemed like he could go wherever I went, the dragon magic that bound us making it possible.

He shrugged. *I think so.*

"Have you seen any of the other competitors?"

He looked a bit confused for a moment, and Poppy poked him.

Daft, Eloise muttered, her little badger face unimpressed.

I looked at her. "Did you speak, Eloise?"

She looked at me innocently, pretending she'd said nothing. Apparently whispered comments were Eloise's thing. That and fighting.

Oh yes. Saw two wolves. Romeo grinned. *Threw pumpkins at them.*

Eloise gave a hissing little laugh, and Poppy joined in.

"Good job. You stay out of trouble, okay? Don't eat too many pumpkins."

He ignored me and took a huge bite, cheeks bulging. Poppy followed suit, chowing down.

I looked at Maximus. "Let's get a move on."

We continued through the graveyard. In the distance, blue glitter exploded into the air.

"The fae are fighting," I whispered, wondering what had attacked them.

"That makes two other teams already in the house. And I'd bet a case of whiskey that the illusionists are here as well."

I chewed my lip, knowing he was right, and searched for the stairs. Where the heck were they?

We kept searching, moving quietly through the graveyard. We'd just come upon a large, slow-moving river when a ghost drifted toward us, looking like it was in slightly better shape than the rest. The figure was human-shaped at least, with a funny hat and a pipe.

I frowned as he neared. Was he...? "Sherlock Holmes?"

The ghost stopped as he neared us. His face was a bit blurry, as if his ghostly form were fading away.

"Indeed." His British accent was clipped and old-sounding, like he'd stepped out of the pages of a musty old book.

Which he had. Sherlock had never really lived, so he couldn't be a ghost. Unless he was the ghost of a story. Either way, I couldn't help the giddy grin that spread over my face.

"And what might you be doing in such a dire place?" he asked.

"We're looking for the ghost in the attic," Maximus said.

"That old bastard?"

"The same," I said. "Do you know how we could get up there? I don't see any stairs. In fact, this doesn't seem like much of a house at all."

"But it is indeed," he said. "Right in the middle of Dartmoor." His gaze brightened. "Have you seen my hound?"

"Heard him," Maximus said.

Sherlock nodded. "For the best. Better that you not run into him. Miserable bugger has a mean bite."

"The stairs?" I prodded.

His gaze sharpened. "Yes, yes. You are in the parlor now. The magic of Dartmoor—and that witch—have overtaken it. But you can get out of here if you cross the bridge."

"Where is it?" Maximus asked.

Sherlock turned and pointed to a spot almost directly behind him. "But there is a trick to it, you see. You must ride over the bridge on the Headless Horseman's stallion."

I frowned. "Wait, what?"

"Steal his horse, ride over the bridge." Sherlock's voice indicated that he thought I was too dumb to live.

"I don't think he's going to like it if we steal his horse," I said. I really didn't want to piss off the locals. I'd read the stories. The Headless Horseman was someone you didn't want as an enemy.

"He's a nasty bloke, so don't worry yourself." He shrugged. "Anyway, it must be done, if you want to reach the attic."

Which, yes, we did.

The sound of thundering hoofbeats sounded from behind us, and Sherlock jumped. "That would be him! Be careful now. He's deadly."

I turned, catching sight of a massive steed galloping toward us. The horse was the biggest I'd ever seen, with a glossy black coat and fangs that overlapped its bottom lip. The eyes burned a fiery red, but it was the headless man who was on top that was really scary. He wore a flowing black cloak and carried a burning jack-o'-lantern under one arm.

My skin chilled.

He raised the fiery pumpkin and hurled his burning cargo straight at our heads.

CHAPTER FIVE

For a split second, I stood frozen, seeing only the massive head-less horseman and the burning pumpkin that hurtled toward me.

Then I snapped out of it and lunged left, diving behind a headstone. Maximus jumped on top of me, shielding me with his body. The pumpkin slammed into the headstone, and the thing exploded, sending shards of stone flying through the air. One hit me on the leg, leaving a slice that burned like hell.

Maximus was off me in a second, and I followed, peering up from behind the ruins of the headstone. The horseman thundered toward us, only forty yards away now. The horse's footsteps made the ground shake, and the man held another burning pumpkin in his hand.

"Ah, crap." I stood, ready to lunge again.

"We need to get that horse," Maximus said.

How? I looked around, searching for any kind of weapon that wouldn't involve getting close. My range with my potion bombs was usually about twenty yards. I didn't want to get that close.

My gaze landed on the river. I looked at Maximus. "I'll slam him off the horse. Can you conjure a net and catch him?"

"I can." He looked back at the headless horseman, who was about to ride between two big trees. "Good plan."

The horseman hurled the pumpkin, and I dived left as it flew for me, a burning orange bomb that looked like a nightmare version of Halloween. I skidded in the dirt, narrowly avoiding the bomb that exploded into the ground, sending up dirt and old bones to rain down upon me.

The horseman was almost through the trees.

This was my moment.

I called on the magic deep within me, dredging it up so I could smash him off his horse. The power surged through my belly, rising up in my chest and out through my limbs. As he rode between the two huge oaks, I commanded the water in the river to rise.

At the same time, right as the Headless Horseman passed the tree trunks, Maximus conjured a giant net that suspended itself between the trunks like a spiderweb.

I forced the water out of the river and toward the horseman, using the skills I'd practiced on stage. They came easier now, and the water shot up, a spear of liquid that slammed into the horseman's chest.

He roared, his big body flying backward off the horse. He slammed into the net, breaking it free from the trees as he flew. When he plowed into the ground, the thing wrapped around him, tangling him up.

For good measure, Maximus conjured another net, this one weighted down by stones. The thing appeared in midair and fell down on the horseman.

"It won't hold him long." Maximus sprinted toward the horse, which was careening toward us. The beast had been running so furiously that it hadn't seemed to notice his master flying off.

Or, more likely, he didn't like his master and just kept running.

With skilled grace, Maximus grabbed the horse's bridle and swung up into the saddle. Clearly, he'd done a lot of horse riding back when he'd lived in ancient times.

He nudged the horse with his heels, and the animal galloped toward me. Maximus leaned over and reached down. I grabbed his hand and jumped. He swung me up behind him in a move so practiced I almost laughed.

How the hell had we just managed *that?*

"Yah!" Maximus commanded, nudging the horse again.

The beast picked up the pace, galloping away on massive hooves.

I turned, spotting the horseman as he rose to his feet and flung off the nets. Another pumpkin had appeared in his hand, and he threw it at us.

I called upon the river again, forcing the water upward and driving it toward the pumpkin. It smashed into the flaming bomb, and the thing exploded, sizzling in midair.

"Almost to the bridge!" Maximus shouted.

"Hurry!"

The horseman conjured another pumpkin, and another, hurling them in quick succession. He was faster than I was, and I missed the third one he threw.

"Duck!" I screamed.

Maximus bent low over the horse, and I followed. The pumpkin whizzed over us, narrowly avoiding the horse's head, and plowed into the ground in front. The earth exploded up in flames, and the horse jumped it, neighing his displeasure.

When we cleared the other side, I spotted the bridge. The

horse's hooves slammed onto the wooden planks as we began to cross.

Oh, thank fates.

Two pale white figures stood on the other side, partially hidden by a large tree.

"Do you see them?" I shouted.

"What?" Maximus's head moved as he looked, but before he could speak, a wall of flame appeared in front of us.

The horse shrieked and rose up on two legs. My heart thudded.

The bridge beneath us began to shake violently, and I looked down at the water. Jagged rocks cut through the water below, which had begun to boil. I turned around. From the other side of the bridge, the Horseman ran at us.

Shit. My stomach churned as the stallion bucked.

The flames in front of us flickered, and through them, I caught another glimpse of a pale white figure.

Wait a second…

The flame wasn't hot. We were so close to the massive wall of fire that I should be burning up. But I wasn't.

"Ride through!" I screamed. "It's an illusion! Natalia and Olga are on the other side."

Maximus laid his hand on the horse's neck to calm it, and somehow, it worked. The animal lowered itself to four feet, then charged. I turned back to find the Headless Horseman, and spotted him almost on the bridge. He sprinted onto it, his footsteps so heavy that they shook the wooden surface even more.

I called upon the water again. Every time I did so, it became easier. I pulled forth a massive wave, slamming it into the bridge and knocking his feet out from under him.

Then the flames swallowed me. The world turned orange and red, but it was no hotter, thank fates.

The horse thundered toward the other side, onto a narrow

road winding through a twisty old forest. I spotted the two illusionists still standing near the large tree, their faces shocked. Before they could move, I pulled a couple of potion bombs from the sack strapped to my back.

One after the other, I hurled the bombs and smashed them into the pale figures. Blue liquid exploded against their chests, my best sleeping potion, and the two women collapsed backward.

"That'll keep them out of our hair for a while," I muttered.

The stallion came to an abrupt stop, bucking wildly.

"Dismount," Maximus said.

The cue from the horse was clear. I scrambled off, Maximus following much more gracefully, and the horse galloped away, heading down the twisty path.

Maximus turned to me. "I can't believe I just rode through fire."

I grinned. "I guess you trust me."

"I must."

White wisps zipped in front of our faces, the magical cameras catching every moment of our connection.

I scowled and swatted out. "Damned things."

"Ignore them." Despite his words, Maximus gave them a withering glance. "Let's get a move on. The fae are back there still. I spotted their magic. But the wolves could be ahead of us."

He was right. I nodded and started forward, headed down the path. It was narrow and made of dirt, while the forest that surrounded us was full of gnarled old trees. Occasionally, I spotted something random like an armchair or an old table and lamp.

"We must be in the living room," I said.

A fat black cat dozed beneath a tree near the path, a bowl of cat food at its side.

"At least the witch takes care of her cats."

The cat opened yellow eyes and hissed at me, but was too lazy to get up. We continued on. My skin prickled with nerves as we walked, my every sense alert.

Up ahead, a section at the side of the path glowed. We slowed as we neared, and I realized that it was a doorway. I edged up to it and peered inside.

It was an old kitchen, and inside, two wolves lay on the ground near the sink, wrapped up in something that looked like toilet paper. I blinked, my gaze darting around the kitchen. It landed on a mummy—one who looked like he'd stepped out of an old horror film.

The mummy's black eyes fell on me.

"Run!" I sprinted past the kitchen door.

Maximus was no dummy—he didn't need to be told twice.

He sprinted alongside me, his pace quick, and we thundered down the path away from the kitchen. One glance behind showed the mummy standing in the glowing light of the door, staring after us.

He didn't pursue, thank fates, no doubt figuring he had enough to handle with the two wolves he'd caught.

Finally, when the mummy was out of sight, we slowed.

Panting, I looked at Maximus. "This place is wild."

"Good entertainment, though."

"Seriously." I searched the path ahead of us, realizing that it looked like it ended. "Come on."

I hurried forward, my heart leaping when I finally spotted a set of stairs. "Jackpot."

They were rickety and old, but they went upward, and that was good enough for me.

I stepped onto the first stair, and the wooden boards shrieked.

"So much for stealth," Maximus said.

Together, we hurried up the stairs, reaching a landing that curved around behind us.

I turned, and my jaw dropped. "Holy fates."

The upstairs was just as big as the downstairs, but this was all open space with wooden bridges crisscrossing the emptiness below. A maze, almost.

"We need to find another set of stairs, straight up to the attic," Maximus said. "They'll be somewhere along the edge, I imagine."

He was right. The space was so big that it was hard to see the edges, especially with the mist that was now rising up from below. We'd have to navigate this weird maze to find the next flight of stairs.

A growl sounded from our left, low and deep. The hair on my arms stood up, and I turned, my heart lodged in my throat.

There was another bridge to our left, about fifteen feet away. Upon it, a massive hound crouched. He was huge—at least seven feet tall at his shoulders. He had to weigh hundreds of pounds. Red eyes blazed, and his lips pulled back from fangs as he snarled.

My stomach plunged and my voice quavered. "Niiiice puppy."

The hound just growled more, and I was one hundred percent sure that we were looking at the Hound of the Baskervilles. Sherlock would be glad to know we'd seen his dog.

Me? Not so much.

"Run!" The word squeaked out of me, and I sprinted away, straight down the bridge and into the mist. Maximus thundered behind me, and the dog growled louder.

A massive thud shook the bridge beneath our feet, and I turned, catching a glimpse of the beast behind Maximus.

It had jumped onto our bridge!

"Get in front of me!" I darted to the side.

"No!"

"Do it!" I put every bit of command into my voice. Dumb man didn't want to put me between him and danger, but *I* was the one with the potion bombs.

His footsteps didn't speed up, and he was probably planning on some hand to hand with that beast from hell. "Fine, then. Catch!"

I dug into my bag of potion bombs and grabbed a super sleeper. It was even stronger than what I'd hit the illusionists with. I tossed it over my shoulder, a nice high arc that he could catch. I glanced back in time to see him snag it out of the air, then whip around and chuck the thing at the hound.

His aim was perfect, and the glass bomb shattered against the beast's chest. The creature roared and slowed, but didn't stop.

Damn it.

Too strong. He wasn't a real dog, that was for sure. He was at least half magic, maybe all, a complicated dark magic spell that would make him impervious to a lot of my potions.

But it *had* slowed him, so it had kind of worked.

"Here's another!" I lobbed another potion bomb at Maximus, which he caught and threw.

Once again the beast only slowed, but at least it didn't jump on us.

The bridge ahead veered left and right, and I took the right, following instinct more than anything else. We sprinted through the strange maze, searching for any kind of stairs to lead us up and out of the mess.

My lungs burned and my muscles ached. I glanced behind, catching sight of the hound, still keeping up. He cut through the mist like a freight train, powerful legs carrying him along despite the colorful potions that were splattered on his chest.

There was no way we would find the stairs with him on our

tails. Not before we were exhausted and out of potion bombs, at least. And when that time came, we'd be doggie chow.

We needed another way out of this.

I looked around, frantic for an answer, but saw only the bridges, cutting endlessly through the wide-open space. They were narrow and rickety, and below, there was nothing but open air. Occasionally, if I looked down at just the right moment, I could spot the graveyard or the twisty little forest. I saw no bursts of blue fae magic, which meant they might already be headed up the stairs.

What if the hound was chasing us when they arrived? They'd dart right past and find the stairs.

We definitely needed another way.

A wild plan popped into my head.

No, it was crazy.

But was it?

Up ahead, our bridge ended right at another. We could turn left or right, but there was nothing ahead except air. Below, I could feel the river. The water called to me, strong and fierce.

Perfect. "We're going over!"

"What?" Maximus shouted, shock in his voice.

"Jump over the edge and trust me."

"Are you crazy?"

"Not about this! Jump straight down, not out!" We were almost there. Just ten feet away, and going fast. There was no more time. Maximus had to follow.

I called upon the river, dragging up as much water as I could manage and praying it was enough. I could see it in my mind's eye, rising up as a thick column, right below where we would jump. With any luck, we'd jump right into it.

I reached the edge of the bridge and leapt over the railing, the air whooshing by my body. I couldn't help the fear that made my stomach drop as I fell. Maximus followed, plummeting behind me. The dog sailed overhead, jumping far out into the air the way four-legged animals generally did.

When the water caught me, elation surged. It closed over my head, cold and shocking, and I began to kick up immediately. It was just a narrow column of water—I didn't want to mistakenly pop out the side of it and start falling through the air again.

I collided with Maximus while shooting for the surface, and together, we made it up. My head burst through, and I gasped, looking around. We were still high up in the air, the column of water like a deep swimming pool. I forced it up some more, carrying us to the level of the bridge above.

With trembling muscles, I climbed onto the bridge. Maximus followed, soaking wet.

I flopped onto my stomach and peered over the edge as I commanded the huge column of water to return to the river. Once the last of it had crashed back into place, I spotted the hound.

He sprinted across the graveyard, chasing one of the ghosts.

Panting, I grinned. "Looks like he's okay."

"That was impressive." Maximus stood, shaking some of the water off like a dog.

I nodded my thanks, but he was right. That had been wild. I was getting really good at this water stuff. Warm pride filled me.

On shaking legs, we inspected our surroundings. With the hound no longer distracting us, I spotted a wall to the left.

I pointed. "Let's go that way."

Together, we tromped across the bridge toward the wall, dripping as we went. Man, being wet sucked.

When we neared the wall and I spotted a narrow staircase, I grinned. "I think we're close."

As we ascended the stairs, the lights began to dim. Each floorboard creaked underfoot, and I couldn't help wincing at the noises.

Tension plucked at every nerve ending as we climbed, the stairway longer than a normal one. But then, everything in this house was weird.

White wisps flitted around our heads as we climbed, and I smacked them away. The scent of dust and mildew grew stronger as we reached the top of the stairs, and when I stepped out into the attic, I was almost disappointed.

It looked just like a normal attic—full of old furniture and boxes. Except when I looked closer, it was pretty damned creepy. To the left was a collection of old dolls with missing eyes—nope, no thanks, not for me—and to the right were four paintings of children in which the feet looked like they were moving.

Pale light gleamed from the ceiling, though where it came from, I had no idea. It glittered on the dust motes in the air, making them sparkle like diamonds.

"Hello?" I called out in a low voice. "Ghost in the attic?"

Only once I'd spoken did I remember that we didn't know if the ghost was friendly.

Eerie silence echoed.

There was no response from the ghost. I hoped we were in the right attic. With our luck, there would be multiple attics. And they'd be filled with poltergeists.

CHAPTER SIX

"Let's look around," I said. The space wasn't huge. Just about the size of a normal house, really. But there were nooks and crannies to be explored.

My heart thudded in a low beat as we began to search the attic. The whole place had a creepy feel to it, enough to make the hair on my arms stand on end. Each creaking floorboard made me jump, and I remembered that this was why I didn't like horror movies.

At one point, I nudged a box with my feet, and a squeak sounded from inside. A familiar squeak.

"Romeo?"

The raccoon's head popped out, and he grinned toothily. In one hand, he held an old postcard with a frayed edge. Poppy's head stuck up next to his, and she was wearing a decrepit old flower behind her ear. No doubt something she'd found up here.

"Where's Eloise?" I asked.

Romeo pointed to the right. *In the chair over there. Too much trash for her lately.*

I turned to see Eloise, who looked impatient as she sat on a dusty chair.

"She's not quite as into trash as you are, is she?"

Romeo shook his head. *She appreciates it well enough, but says we need to eat fresh bugs sometimes. Doesn't appreciate the joy in finding the gold in the muck.*

I smiled. Eloise was the responsible party, it seemed. "Well, stay out of trouble."

Romeo gave me a shocked look, and Poppy tittered disapprovingly.

We would never get in trouble.

"Sure, sure, Romeo." He was a smooth talker, that one, but I wasn't falling for it.

I left him to continue scouting out the boxes and continued on. Tension thrummed across my skin as I searched, and at one point, I ended up in a small nook with Maximus. He was the only thing that smelled fresh and clean in here, and I liked it. A lot.

We were standing only a couple feet apart when he spoke in a low voice. "There's no ghost up here."

Maybe it was the quiet of the attic, or the calm after the storm of running from the Headless Horseman and the Hound of the Baskervilles, but his voice sent warmth rushing through me. Probably it was the fact that we were so close. My nerve endings perked up, and I shivered, leaning a bit closer to him.

A white light flitted in front of my face.

One of the wisps.

I scowled and batted it away, but was glad it had made an appearance. I didn't need to be distracted by Maximus right now.

A pale light from the right caught my eye, and I turned.

A ghostly white figure was drifting out of the wall. It floated just above the ground in the corner, the figure of a man. He was in better shape than most of the other ghosts, with a distinct human form and very little fraying at the edges.

I turned toward him, my spine tingling. "Are you the ghost in the attic?"

He said nothing, but his mouth seemed to be moving.

I glanced at Maximus, confused. He shrugged.

Together, we approached on silent feet. As we neared, I realized that his mouth *was* moving. He was talking, just too quietly to really hear. There was a constant whisper, but not something I could decipher.

I got up as close as I could, standing only a couple feet from him. This near, I could see that he was a man in his later years, with a bushy mustache and clothes that looked to be from the late nineteenth or early twentieth century.

"Can you read lips?" I asked Maximus.

"No."

The ghost looked annoyed that we couldn't understand, his brow furrowed and lips moving faster. What the hell was he saying?

Crap, we'd made it all this way and were missing the important stuff. Could a ghost write? Maybe that way, he could pass his message on to us.

I turned around to look for a pen, even though I knew he probably couldn't hold the thing. My eye caught on an old gramophone in the corner, the big brass cone extending far into the air.

Hmmmm.

I hurried over and grabbed it, detaching the cone from the old wooden player, then returned to Maximus and the ghost.

"I'm just going to hold this up in front of your face to amplify your voice," I warned him, not wanting him to think I was attacking and strike back. Or worse, stop talking.

The ghost looked skeptical, but he nodded.

I raised the gramophone, and he leaned toward it. "Can you hear me?"

The whisper was deathly quiet, but I could just barely make out the words. My heart leapt. Maybe we'd get out of here soon. "Yes. Are you the ghost in the attic?"

"I suppose I am."

"Who are you?" Maximus asked.

"The ghost of Christmas past."

"Wait, what?" I frowned. "Really?"

"No." He looked at me like I was an idiot, and maybe I was. "I'm Sir Arthur Conan Doyle."

"Oh." I blinked. "The writer of Sherlock and *The Hound of the Baskervilles.*"

"The very same." He beamed proudly.

"Your dog is causing some chaos down below," Maximus said.

It didn't seem possible, but his proud smile grew even larger. "He's something, isn't he?"

"That's one word for it," I said. "Why are you here?"

"It quite suits me. This is my moor, as I like to think of it. And this is the hotel where I stayed while I wrote *The Hound of the Baskervilles*, though magic and time have taken their toll. Not to mention that witch. When she moved in, everything really went downhill."

"Yeah, she's a piece of work," I said.

"Avoid Bertha. She'll put you in a soup."

"Good advice," Maximus said, and I almost laughed at his wry tone.

"We're here for a clue," I said. "The Intermagic Games have chosen your house as a location for one of their challenges."

"Yes, you are not the first to come."

I frowned. Oh shit. I swore I'd seen the fae, the wolves, and the illusionists downstairs. We'd beaten them here. Which meant only one thing.

"Who arrived before us?" Maximus asked.

"Two women," Sir Arthur whispered. "Dark hair and purple eyes."

Damn it. "Purple eyes?"

"Strangest ones I've ever seen."

I looked at Maximus. "The witches."

He nodded, then looked at Sir Arthur. "How long ago were they here? Can you tell us anything about them?"

He shrugged. "Nothing to tell. They came and collected a map from that far wall."

He pointed, and I turned to see that there were three maps against the far wall, with a space for a fourth that was now missing.

"When?" I demanded.

"Twenty minutes ago, or so."

Damn it. They were long gone.

Footsteps thundered up the stairs, followed by an angry screech. I turned back to Sir Arthur and Maximus, eyes wide.

"The witch!" Sir Arthur said. "Hurry!"

I didn't need to be told twice. I spun and sprinted to the wall, then yanked down one of the maps. Maximus positioned himself between me and the entrance where the witch would appear.

Man, the map was big. I started rolling it, but it was slow progress.

"Just fold it and go!" Sir Arthur shouted. "I'll hold her off!"

The witch burst through at that moment, her hair and eyes wild. She shrieked her rage when she saw us. "Trespassers!"

"You old biddy!" Sir Arthur shouted. He raised his arms, and objects began to fly into the air. Furniture and boxes, old lamps and picture frames. The box containing Romeo and Poppy floated up, and their little heads peeked out.

Time for action! Romeo jumped out of his box and leapt onto a chair that floated halfway to the ceiling. He grabbed a small figurine of a dancing shepherdess and hurled it at the witch. Poppy joined in, as did Eloise, who finally looked happy. Any opportunity to rampage pleased Eloise.

They drove the witch away from the exit, allowing us a path to safety.

The witch shot a blast of dark gray magic from her hands. It looked like tar as it hurtled through the air and smashed apart a lamp that was flying toward her head.

Yep, better avoid the witch's tar blasts. Whatever was in that stuff looked deadly.

"Come on." Maximus spun and sprinted for the door, clearing a path for us by shoving aside heavy furniture that floated in the air.

I followed, keeping my eye on the witch as she tried to plow through the floating furniture to get to us. Her black tar magic blasted apart a chair, and I dived low, avoiding the large flying splinters.

We reached the stairs and raced down. As I ran, I folded the map and shoved it into my inner pocket, hoping it wouldn't get too wet from my clothes.

"Go right at the bottom!" Sir Arthur's voice sounded from behind us. I tucked the info away, hoping it was a shortcut.

From behind, the witch shrieked her rage. The sound of a happy hiss followed, and it had to be Poppy or Eloise. I landed on the next level with a thud and sprinted along the bridge, following Maximus.

We weren't the only ones on the bridge this time. The Hound of the Baskervilles was chasing the fae across a bridge at the other side, while the two wolves were sprinting toward us.

Ah, crap.

Maximus veered left, taking another bridge to avoid them.

The hound must have figured out that we had a map,

74

because he left the fae and thundered toward us. Or maybe he was still pissed about the trick we pulled on him.

"Faster!" I shouted at Maximus, though I probably couldn't have gone any quicker myself.

But the hound was gaining.

My lungs burned as we raced across the bridges, going left and right in our search for the exit stairs. I glanced behind to see the hound closing in, his black fur gleaming and his fangs dripping.

I shoved a hand into my potion bag and pulled out a bomb. I didn't even look to see what it was, just lobbed it over my shoulder at the hound. The glass popped as it broke against the hound, and I glanced back to see the beast slow, just temporarily.

"Stairs ahead!" Maximus said.

Thank fates. My lungs and legs were about to give out.

As I stepped onto the first stair, I looked behind. The hound still followed us, and it seemed the wolves had joined in.

Oh, those bastards. They probably thought it would be easier to take the map from us than to continue on through the challenges. How the heck they knew we had a map, I had no idea.

I turned back and clattered down the stairs, going so fast I nearly fell. At the bottom, Maximus and I turned right, avoiding the mummy in the kitchen and hopefully the graveyard as well.

We sprinted through a cluttered little hall, dodging tables full of knickknacks and far too many umbrella stands. This was the weirdest freaking place.

The floor beneath our feet began to rumble, as if an earthquake were tearing apart the moor. My legs wobbled, and I almost lost my footing. Desperate, I grabbed onto the wall, pushing myself off and sprinting forward. The hound's footsteps thundered on the floor behind us, and crashes sounded as he knocked over curio cabinets and umbrella stands.

I peeked back to see the hound only twenty feet away. The two wolves were right behind him, their lips peeled back from their teeth in a snarl.

Yep, this sucked.

"There's a door ahead," Maximus shouted.

It loomed in the distance, welcoming despite the peeling black paint. Was this the front door?

Shit, if it was, there were massive chains strapped over the front. Perfect for keeping people in rather than keeping them out.

We'd be trapped there, trying to get out, while the hound and wolves slammed into us.

Desperate, I dug into my potion bag and rooted around. There weren't many left, but when my fingertips brushed over a triangular shaped one, hope exploded within me.

I yanked it out and shouted, "Maximus, duck!"

He bent at the waist as he ran, giving me just enough time to hurl my potion bomb. The triangular glass bomb flipped through the air as it hurtled toward the door. It smashed against it, and the whole thing disintegrated, chains and all.

We sprinted out onto the front steps, the night air fresh and cold compared to the stuffy house. I ran down the stairs after Maximus, looking behind. The hound plowed out after us, the wolves following.

Crap.

I pushed myself harder, no longer feeling the pain in my legs and lungs but knowing it was there. It wouldn't have surprised me if I had just suddenly run out of energy and fell over with no warning.

"Almost there!" Maximus shouted.

We just had to get past the pumpkin patch in order to use the transport charm.

I sprinted into the pumpkin patch, avoiding the bigger squash and glancing behind to see that the hound had stopped right at the edge of the pumpkins.

Hell yeah!

Something tightened around my ankle.

Oh crap.

I had one brief, flaring thought before the vines yanked me toward the ground.

"Maximus!" I lunged for him as I went down, arm outstretched. Somehow, I knew we shouldn't be separated. Not with the vines dragging us down.

He was trapped, too, up to his knees. He reached for me, and our hands clasped. I gripped him like the lifeline he was, but when the vines pulled us harder, wrapping around our legs like snakes, I realized that maybe even he couldn't get us out of here.

The vines worked quickly, twining around our bodies and squeezing tight. Panic flared in my chest. A vine closed over my eyes.

Blackness.

I screamed, thrashing as hard as I could.

But the vines were too tight. They gripped so hard I couldn't breathe. I tightened my hold on Maximus, unable to help myself.

The weight on top of me grew heavier. More vines were burying us. We would be trapped, dying beneath a pile of vegetation.

I could feel every inch of them, twisting and crushing and squeezing. They glowed with life, so strongly that I could almost feel it. I wanted to suck it into me, to use their strength as my own and break free.

Use it. The voice echoed in my head, strong and fierce. *Use it.*

Use it? But how?

Magic swelled in my chest, bright and dark at the same time. It was so weird that it almost made me queasy. I could feel the vines even more strongly now, though. Not just the strength of their grip, but *them*. Their essence, or something.

Take their power. Use it. Send them to the underworld.

What the heck?

But I listened to the voice, going on instinct. This had to be another Dragon God power, and damned if I was going to let it go. Not if it could save our lives.

The magic had swelled so much inside of me that I felt like my skin would burst. I pushed it out toward the vines, uncertain of what would happen.

When their grip on me weakened, elation surged through me. I gasped, sucking in air, as the vines began to wither. I fed more of the magic to them, pushing it into the vines.

Only once I could see the moon again—once I could breathe again—did I realize that this magic was *killing* the vines.

Oh crap, I didn't need any part of that.

At least, I didn't need anyone to *know* that I could do that. It was a kind of death magic, and the Order of the Magica obviously didn't like people possessing that kind of magic.

I struggled to pull the magic back into myself, trying to hide it from the wisps. Hide it from the world.

I'd killed enough of the vines that we could escape. Maximus was already breaking free next to me.

It took everything I had to suck the magic back into me. I imagined it as a net that I was pulling back from the sea, dragging it toward me so it wouldn't touch any more vines.

It worked, and eventually I felt all of it recede back inside of me. As I stood, stronger and more refreshed than I had been, I realized that I'd also pulled in energy.

I sucked in a breath, feeling strong. Powerful.

Oh fates.

Had I taken some of the plant's energy for my own? Had I taken what belonged to another living thing?

Somehow, I knew that this wasn't plant magic. It wasn't the vegetation itself that I was connected to—not in the way that my sister Ana was connected to plants. Or the way my friend Nix was.

It was the *life* in the plant. I'd killed the plant and taken the energy.

I shuddered, horrified.

"Rowan! We need to go." Maximus's voice broke through my haze, and I realized he might have been calling for a while. He was tugging on my hand, too.

We'd never let go of each other, but I'd been so panicked I hadn't even noticed.

I shoved away the thoughts of my scary new magic and ran for it, following Maximus out of the pumpkin patch and toward the moor.

The wisps flittered around my head, trying to get a good view of me as I ran. Fear iced my skin.

Everyone had seen me. They'd all seen the death magic. Had they connected it with me? Did the Order of the Magica now have plans to toss me in the Prison for Magical Miscreants?

The sound of low growls sounded from behind.

I glanced back, catching sight of the wolves who had leapt over the dead vines and were still chasing us. Oh, shit.

I turned back and ran faster.

CHAPTER SEVEN

"We're almost to the border!" Maximus dug into his pocket as he ran and withdrew a transport charm.

I glanced behind. The wolves were closer. Only ten feet behind us. So close I could see the whites of their eyes and count their fangs. Fates, I could almost smell their breath.

I turned back and sprinted faster. Maximus hurled the transport charm to the ground, and a burst of glittery gray magic exploded upward.

We lunged into it, side by side, as the wolves snapped at us from behind.

Oh please don't let them be able to follow.

I stumbled out onto a quiet city street as dawn broke over the horizon, Maximus at my side. I spun, ready to fight. My heart thundered in my ears as I searched for the wolves.

They didn't appear.

I sagged, panting. "Oh, thank fates."

"Opportunistic bastards," Maximus muttered. "Trying to steal our map instead of going for their own."

"The other contestants are as big of a threat as the challenges." Slowly catching my breath, I stood and inspected the city street. It looked like an older part of London where modern buildings sat next to older ones. "Where are we?"

"Supernatural district of London. I live here. It was the first place I thought of, and I didn't know if the Protectorate wanted those wolves on their doorstep."

A smile tugged at my mouth. "I think they'd enjoy the challenge."

"You're probably right. Come on." He gestured for me to follow, and I did, crossing the street behind him as the white wisps flitted behind. I batted them away, annoyed at their constant presence.

Annoyed, and afraid.

I'd had my dark magic under control. I'd never expected to get *more* of it. And a Dragon God power, at that. All of my sisters' Dragon God powers were good powers. Or neutral, at least.

I shook away the worry and followed Maximus to a narrow stone building. He unlocked a heavy wooden door with ornate carvings that looked like a private entrance of some kind, and it led into a beautiful, quiet lobby. Whatever this building had been, it was old. But in a fancy way. Like a nineteenth century government building.

Maximus shut the door behind him, stopping the wisps from entering. I wasn't sure on the rules on them entering private domains, but Maximus didn't seem willing to let them. I turned to inspect the building. The little lobby contained two elevators, and Maximus took the one on the right.

The ride up was silent and quick. Both of us caught our breath. My clothes stuck wetly to me, and I shifted, miserable. I hadn't noticed while I was still running for my life, but now it was a pain in the tail.

The elevator stopped, and we stepped out into small foyer. He unlocked a door, then led me into a living room with windows that overlooked the city. Yellow lights gleamed like diamonds in the distance, thousands of homes and shops welcoming the day. A brilliant orange sunset shined through the many windows. The furniture was good quality but simple.

"Wow, this is nice." I spun around. An open door gave a peek of the kitchen, and another showed a big computer sitting on a desk. I'd wondered how he would live. "Not very much like what I expected."

"I like the modern age." A smile quirked up at the edge of his mouth. "It's a good change from rural Germany and the Colosseum."

I remembered what he'd said about being abducted as a boy from a village in Germany around the turn of the millennia and sent to the Colosseum in Rome to be a gladiator. Yes, this had to be much better. And now that I thought of it, this place made a lot of sense.

"You've certainly put the past behind you."

He rubbed his chin. "It's a past meant to be left behind. I wasn't close with my family. And the Colosseum... Well, I'm sure you can imagine."

I nodded, able to picture the misery all too well.

"I can remake myself here," he said. "And I like that."

I pointed to the computer in the little office. "And you're stepping into the present, it seems."

"Ah, that. Well, I try." A rueful smile stretched across his face, and suddenly he wasn't the super deadly gladiator I'd come to know and lust after. He was just a guy. A handsome, powerful, rich guy. But just a guy. "Not going quite as I'd hoped. I don't have the knack for it."

"They're overrated anyway." Chilly, I tugged off my wet leather jacket.

He stepped forward and took it from me. "You need dry clothes." His magic swelled briefly, and then a set of clothes that were identical to mine appeared in his hands. He handed them to me, and I grinned. "You can change into those upstairs. Then let's look at the map. We have a short while before the others catch up."

I nodded, spotting the wisps outside the windows. Damned things hadn't managed to follow us in, but they certainly weren't leaving me alone.

Maximus showed me to a staircase that led up, and I realized that his place was really a lot like mine. Much bigger and not full of potions and crap, but a similar layout.

His room was simple, with a massive bed covered in a gray duvet. The scent of him was everywhere—cedar and soap and that uniquely wonderful scent of his skin. I took a deep breath, just once, then tried to ignore it.

Wisps floated in front of the windows outside, and I stalked over and pulled the window shade down. Annoying little jerks. Since I couldn't bear to take longer than necessary with that map waiting, I skipped the big marble shower and tugged on the clothes he'd given me, then pressed my fingertips to my comms charm.

"Bree? Ana?" I murmured.

The connection crackled, and Bree's voice came through. "Rowan! How are you?"

"Still in the lead."

"Are you safe?" Ana asked. "Injured?"

"Nope. Not yet. But those damned witches beat us to the first clue. A map."

"Damn it," Ana cursed.

"Be careful around them," Bree said. "We'll update Jude that you've seen them."

"Thanks. Any word on the electric sword, Bree? Was your guy able to enchant it?" I asked.

"Yes." I could hear the smile in Bree's voice. "It's in the ether. Call on it if you need it."

"Thanks. Love you guys."

"Love you back." They spoke in unison, and I smiled.

I cut the connection and tossed my wet clothes in the laundry room that was off the bedroom. I grabbed the map we'd gotten from the attic in the haunted house, then hurried down the stairs. As I passed a table near the door to the living room, I caught sight of a massive pile of gold.

"Whoa." The word escaped me before I could help it.

Maximus looked up from where he stood in the middle of the living room, clearly having just changed into fresh clothes.

I shot him an impressed look. No other conjurer I'd ever met could conjure gold or money. "If you can do that, why don't you just do it all the time?"

He shook his head. "It takes a lot of energy. I can make enough to buy pretty much anything I want." He gestured to the amazing apartment that had to be really expensive. "But I like to work for the things I own. I do make some for charities, though. I can't make enough to upset the balance of the world economy —that'd take me hundreds of years, probably."

That was good, at least. "What charities?"

He shrugged, turning toward the kitchen. His voice turned gruff. "Kids, animals, environment."

Those seemed like good ones. I smiled, liking Maximus even more. I had to bet he chose kids because he'd had a shitty childhood. Animals because he was a decent dude. And the environment because I imagined it looked a whole lot different now than it had in his day. I kept all my assumptions to myself, though. He didn't seem like the sort to want to discuss his motivations.

"Food?" he asked.

"Oh my fates, yes." My stomach grumbled, as if it suddenly remembered it was hungry.

The kitchen was bright and modern, but the fridge was mostly bare.

"I'm not much for cooking." He pulled sandwich stuff out of the fridge and I grinned.

"Fine by me. Neither am I."

We threw together some quick sandwiches and drank water out of the tap. He must have been on the move so much between his work for the Order and training me that he was low on supplies. Unless he conjured them all and just didn't care to keep a full fridge. I was so damned hungry that I probably could have eaten a sandwich made of sawdust and tires.

As I polished off the sandwich, I unfolded the map on the counter and stared. Out of the corner of my eye, I realized that the white wisps were shining through the windows, determined to get a good view for the audience. But I was too entranced to care.

At first, the map made no sense. Just squiggly lines. Then I realized that part of it was glowing slightly.

I pressed my fingertip to the brighter spot on the map, and magic flared. The paper shined, and an envelope burst forth, appearing out of thin air.

Maximus stiffened. I grabbed the envelope, which was made of a heavy ivory paper, and carefully opened it.

"Feels a hell of a lot like an invitation." I unfolded it and nodded. "Yep. We're invited to Cinderella's royal ball."

"Cinderella? The fairy tale?"

"The very same." I looked at the map, realizing now that the glowing spot had been the destination. It no longer glowed, and it was easier to make out the details. "The Royal Palace of South London. There's a Royal Palace in South London? Does the queen know about that?"

"Supernatural," he said. "It's here, in the supernatural district."

85

"Ah. Never been." Besides my time with the Protectorate and the occasional adventures to help Bree and Ana with their work there, I hadn't seen a lot of the world. Alaska as a kid, then whatever states we passed through to reach Death Valley. Then Scotland.

"What time?"

"Seven p.m., tonight." My shoulders relaxed, gratitude flowing through me. "We get a rest."

"Good. We could use one." His gaze sharpened on the envelope. "There will be a lot of guests. With those two purple-eyed witches on the loose, we should get backup."

"Want me to ask the Protectorate? Or do you have people at the Order you want to bring in?" I hated that idea, honestly.

"Better to use the Protectorate. They're skilled and I trust them more."

"Really?"

"I'm not an idiot." He grinned. "They're tough and smart."

"That they are. I'll call and ask." Maximus waited while I pressed my fingertips to the comms charm again and told my sisters what was up. They promised to go to Jude and then update me with their progress.

I cut the connection and flipped the invitation over. On the back was a beautiful illustration of a woman's shoe. It sparkled like glass. Beneath it, in a scrolling text, read the words *Find me.*

"Cinderella's glass slipper," I said.

"It's the next clue. We must have to find it."

I frowned. "I guess so."

Maximus's gaze turned serious, and I swallowed hard. When he spoke, I wasn't surprised by the words. I'd been waiting for them. "How did we get out of the pumpkin patch? That wasn't my magic."

I looked toward the windows, where the wisps flittered, and lowered my voice to a whisper. No way I could let those things hear me. He leaned close to listen, and I could feel the heat of him.

"New magic," I murmured. "Dragon God magic. I killed the plants."

"The power of death?"

I shrugged, miserable inside. "I don't know."

"Is it linked to the darkness that was inside you already?"

I shook my head, my hair brushing against his shoulder. "I don't think so. It feels new. Different. The plant's life force flowed into me, making me stronger."

"That's very useful."

My heart thundered, and panic gripped me with cold claws. "I don't want that power. Death magic is dangerous. The Order of the Magica forbids it."

He nodded, his gaze serious. "You need to learn to control it."

"But I don't *want* it." I was just mad. At the world. At myself. First I got the dark magic from my time with the Rebel Gods, and now this—death magic as one of my Dragon God powers.

Is there something about me that attracts this?

"It's not all bad, Rowan." Maximus's gaze searched mine. "Death is the other side of the coin of life. It's natural."

"But it's dangerous."

"You were already dangerous. You could whip up a potion that would kill a man in a second. And the way you use your sword? It's the same."

"It's something the Order frowns on."

"And we're going to have to be careful with that. A bunch of old men with too much to fear. If you practice and learn to control it, they never need to know."

It was the story of my life, but I didn't want to think about it. Instead, I focused on the hand that I'd laid on the table. Maximus's larger hand moved to cover mine, and my vision narrowed in on it. His palm was hot and hard, strong and calloused. It dwarfed my own, and my breath caught.

Prickles of awareness traveled all the way up my arm to my neck, then down the rest of my body. Every inch of me tingled.

How the hell could a simple touch feel like that?

Even my breathing was weird. Slow and hard. Tunnel vision narrowed my line of sight, until all I could see was where we touched.

"Do it." His voice was low, rough.

Do what?

What were we talking about?

"Practice your magic. On me."

Practice? All I could think about was his lips. His hands.

"You drew life from those plants until they withered. I'm a hell of a lot stronger than a pumpkin vine. So draw energy from me. I can always pull back if it's too much."

Why would he pull away? This was too good.

Then my mind caught on the first words he'd said. Awareness crashed back into me, driving away sexy thoughts of what he could do with his hands.

We weren't flirting.

He was trying to get me to kill him.

My gaze flicked up to his. At first, I thought maybe there was the briefest flare of heat in his deep blue eyes.

"No. I'm not going to try to kill you." But I didn't move my hand out from under his. I was too weak.

"Not kill me." His smile suggested that I was a moron, but somehow, he suggested it in a nice way. Which wasn't possible, so clearly this was all my hormones talking. "Just practice drawing power."

I wanted to draw a smile out of him. A kiss. Not power.

Because despite his moronic idea, I was still seriously feeling the connection between us. I wanted to just lean forward and press my lips to his. It'd be amazing, I already knew. The most amazing kiss ever.

Behind him, a white light flitted by the window, then zipped through, somehow sneaking through a crack at the base. It flew over to hover by his head.

I blinked and leaned back. "Shit."

CHAPTER EIGHT

Maximus blinked and turned to face the wisp. A fierce scowl creased his features. He pulled his hand out from under mine, and I mourned the loss. With a quick shove back from the table, he stood and reached out for the wisp.

He was so quick that his hand closed around the thing in a flash. He carried it to the window, where more wisps were trying to get in through the tiny gap their fellow had found.

He spoke directly through the glass, his voice hard. "I've tried to humor your rules and let these damned wisps follow. I even let them spy through the window. But entering my home is too much. Begone until the beginning of the next challenge."

His voice was so hard, so serious, that it sent a shiver down my spine. I should have focused on the fact that he said *begone* like the old-school gladiator dude that he was, but it was his tone that got me.

It got the wisps, too. They zipped away.

He opened the window and flung the other out, then slammed it shut and pulled the curtains. When he turned back to me, he frowned. "Miserable things."

I nodded, just staring at him. I was a total ninny, but his toughness just made me want him more.

What a moron.

"Let's keep practicing," he said.

"We never started."

"We'll start now."

"I'm *not* practicing on you."

He sighed, frustration evident in the tenseness of his muscles and the crease of his brow. "Fine. Then you need to practice on something. Just so you can see that this magic isn't evil."

"It *is*."

"Accept that death isn't evil, Rowan. It can be used by evil and for evil, but in itself, death is not evil. It's not the same as the dark magic that poisoned you before. I can feel it."

He was right, though. I could feel it, too. The power terrified me—it was just so dangerous to have—but maybe it wasn't evil. It didn't feel as dark as the other magic had, at least.

Anxiety shivered over my skin, making it feel too tight, but I nodded. "Fine. I'll practice on a plant, then."

The tiniest smile quirked at the corner of his mouth, so little that I wasn't even sure I'd seen it. He went to the corner of the kitchen and picked up a little plant from the windowsill.

I frowned at it. "I really don't want to kill your basil."

"Is that what this is?" He looked at it appraisingly. "I just thought it smelled nice. And the idea of bringing plants inside... Well, it was foreign to me."

"The modern age is wild," I said wryly.

He set the plant down on the table and returned to his seat. He was a couple of feet away now, not nearly as close as when I'd been whispering to him about my magic, but I could still smell him. Still feel him.

It took everything I had to drag my attention away. I focused on the plant, touching a fingertip to it. Maximus was right. If I had this in me, I really needed to learn to use it. Maybe I could one day get rid of it, but until I had the time to figure that out, I needed to learn to control it.

The plant felt fresh and green under my fingertip. I had no idea how I could *feel* the greenness of it, but somehow I could. It meant life to me, and it flowed up my fingertip and into my arm.

I yanked my finger back, panting.

Had I controlled that? Had I pulled the life out of it?

I shook my head to clear it, then pressed my fingertip to the plant again, trying to repel the life force that I felt within.

It worked. No tingles flowed up my arm, no greater sense of strength. A wobbly smile stretched across my face.

"Take power from it," Maximus said.

I wasn't sure if that was his nice way of saying "kill it," but I decided not to focus on that. I would take just a tiny bit.

I imagined the death magic within me as a bottle locked tight with a cork. I loosened the cork, accessing just a tiny bit of the death magic. Letting myself feel the life in the plant.

The magic burst to the surface, sucking the power out of the plant. It flowed up my arm like raw energy, and the plant withered.

I yanked my arm back. "Damn it!"

"You did well."

"I did it too fast. I was trying to only take a little. I need more control."

"You'll get it."

"I want to give this power back. I thought I'd escaped having dark magic that randomly killed."

"You did. This isn't random, and it's not dark. It's just part of life."

"The shitty part."

A wry smile tugged at his lips, making him look impossibly handsome. "I won't argue with that."

"I just miss the days when I had my original magic. When it was just me and my sisters in the desert, kicking ass and taking names."

"What was your original power?"

"Telekinesis." I shrugged, bittersweet just thinking of it. "Nothing iffy about tossing things around in the air."

If I ever talked to a shrink, they'd probably tell me that was one of the reasons I didn't like Lavender. She had the power I'd lost.

"What happened to it?" he asked.

"The Rebel Gods took it when I was their captive. They used the raw magical energy for some really bad shit and put some of their own dark magic into me. It's a mess, really."

"You never got it back?"

"It's locked in a rock. My sisters saved it for me. But the power inside is polluted. I can never take it back." I stood, suddenly frustrated. "And it doesn't matter. Now that I'm getting my Dragon God magic, I would have lost my original magic anyway. It's just how it works. Dragon God magic is so powerful that it shoves out your other magic."

"But you still miss it." He stood to join me, close enough that I could reach out and touch him.

"I probably always will." I shook my head slightly, trying to drive off the sadness. "But there's no point in moping. I'm really damned lucky. I know that."

He stepped closer, his hands flexing as if he wanted to touch me.

I wanted him to touch me.

"You have power inside of you, Rowan," he said. "Massive amounts of it. I can feel it. You're strong. Amazingly so. Your original magic might be gone, but it doesn't make you any lesser. Your experiences, dark as they've been, only make you stronger."

I swallowed hard at the tone of his voice. It was as if he was trying to force his own belief into me. To make me believe in myself.

I looked up at him, swaying slightly toward him, unable to stop myself. He seemed to sway toward me as well. There was a live wire connecting us. Though we touched nowhere, it felt like we touched everywhere.

Time slowed. His dark gaze, hot and intense, met mine. My lips parted.

The wisps were gone. They couldn't interrupt.

And he smelled so good. His scent twined around me, making my head swirl. I leaned even closer.

Someone pounded on the front door.

I jumped, flying back from him. "Holy crap."

He frowned, annoyed, and looked up at the door. "I never have visitors."

"Order of the Magica and Representative of the Intermagic Games. Open up!"

Horror opened a gaping hole in my chest. I could actually feel the blood rush from my cheeks. No way, no way, no way. My gaze flashed to Maximus's.

His was calm and steady. Anchoring me.

He reached out and squeezed my arm, then leaned close to whisper at my ear. Just in case any of them had super senses, probably, but I liked the feel of his breath. "Don't worry. We don't know why they're here. And there are only two."

"You're sure?"

He tapped his ear. "Killer senses."

"Do you know the Order of the Magica guy?" I asked.

He shook his head. "Totally different department. He's in

Magical Enforcement. I doubt he even knows about the witches infiltrating the competition."

Magical Enforcement. I swallowed hard.

"We haven't informed the Intermagic Games about the infiltrators," Maximus said. "But I may do it now. We have confirmation that they are in the game, so it's time. It might also distract them from you."

I nodded, my head buzzing. "Do we have to let them in?"

"I think it's wisest."

"What if they're here because they saw my death magic on the competition?" It had to be that.

"They don't know you caused that. You were buried beneath the vines. It's best to let them in and play dumb. We'll throw them off the scent. And if we don't, then we'll take them out. But no need to go straight to running."

Straight to running.

I hated running. After a childhood spent doing that, I didn't want to return to it. The idea hardened my spine. Maximus's plan was solid. I wouldn't run.

Stiffly, I nodded.

He strode to the door. As he reached for the handle, my heart began to pound.

He swung open the door to reveal two men. Each was slight and pale, and I'd have sworn they were brothers if not for the vastly different features. One looked a bit like a cocker spaniel, and the other like a rat. The rat man was the same as the one we'd met at the beginning of the Intermagic Games, I realized. He'd never introduced himself, though.

They both had strong magic, and it rolled over me in waves, smelling like a pile of fresh laundry and a cup of strong tea, respectively.

"Rowan Blackwood and Maximus Valerius?" said the cocker spaniel.

"You're at the right place," Maximus said.

The cocker spaniel stuck out his hand. "I'm Harry Ward, representative of the Order of the Magica."

The rat held out his hand next. "And I'm Oliver Keates, Intermagic Games."

"What are you doing here?" Maximus didn't waste any time, it seemed. "We need to rest up before the next competition."

Oliver nodded, looking like a nice rodent, at least. His demeanor had changed since earlier. He was no longer bossy and rude. Maybe he was playing good cop. "Of course, of course."

Harry Ward, the cocker spaniel, cleared his throat, and it was suddenly clear that he was the mean cop. "We're here about the withering of the pumpkin vines at the haunted house on Dartmoor."

Oliver stepped forward. "It wasn't part of the competition. It had to have been something you did to them."

A low shriek sounded in my head—pure fear—and I stiffened, trying not to reveal a single bit of my emotions. The last thing they needed was to see how freaked out I was. There was no way I was going to survive all the other miserable shit in my past and let a mean cocker spaniel get me in the end.

A quick glance at Maximus showed him opening his lips to speak. With horror, I realized that he might be about to take the blame.

Oh, hell no.

"A potion," I said quickly. "I'm a potions master."

Harry the cocker spaniel frowned. "A potion that wilts vines until they die? That was widespread death you caused there, young lady."

"*Young lady*?" My anger echoed in my voice, so strong that even I wouldn't want to get on my bad side.

The cocker spaniel winced. "I'm sorry. That wasn't politically correct."

I barked a harsh laugh. "Politically correct? That's just a way of saying not being an asshole. And you, sir, are an asshole."

He bristled, and I winced internally. Okay, it was one thing to get pissed; it was entirely another to make enemies of the man who had the keys to the Prison for Magical Miscreants. If he didn't believe me, I'd be in damned big trouble.

"We're going to need a sample of your potion, Ms. Blackwood. If it is indeed just a potion, we'll apologize for your wasted time."

I nodded sharply, even though I didn't have a potion like that and had never made anything like it. Sucking the life out of plants on such a large scale was rare. "I used the last of it up, but when the competition is over, I can get you a sample."

"We're not keen on waiting that long."

I looked at Oliver, the Intermagic Games guy. "What do you say, boss? Shall we take a break from the competition so I can whip up a sample of my potion?"

Oliver shifted uncomfortably, his nose twitching. "Well, we really don't have the time. And you two are favorites of the viewers." He looked at Harry. "Can it wait until after?"

Harry's eyes narrowed, and I regretted my earlier outburst even more. But it was better than groveling, I reminded myself. *That* I would never do.

"Fine," Harry snapped. "But my office will be expecting a sample of this potion."

I nodded, trying to look bored. "I'll have it to you ASAP." And since being insolent seemed to be my calling card with old Harry, I drew an X over my chest. "Cross my heart and hope to die."

He frowned at that, then turned.

"Wait." Maximus's voice halted him mid stride. "There's another issue."

Harry turned back to face us, while Oliver just widened his eyes.

"We believe there were two unauthorized competitors in the race at the haunted house. They reached the map before we did. They're dangerous."

Oliver nodded, turning slightly green. "We're aware. They are indeed unauthorized interlopers, but we've guaranteed they cannot get to the final prize."

Maximus nodded, clearly not convinced. "They could do great damage if they got their hands on that prize."

"They cannot." Oliver twisted his hands. "There's nothing we can do about them at this stage—they have the clue about the next phase, just like you do. But we'll ensure they can't touch the final prize."

"You can't cancel that phase?" asked the cocker spaniel.

I wanted to kick him. Of course we didn't want the games cancelled. We needed to track these witches and figure out what their deal was. But Maximus was right. He was from a totally different department and had no idea what was going on with the witches.

Oliver shook his head. "Too much money, too much planning. And you agreed to participate even though it was deadly. So just be careful."

I almost scoffed, but managed to keep my mouth shut at the last minute.

They left a few moments later, and Maximus shut the door. I sagged against the chair behind me and scrubbed my hand over my face.

"Do you have a potion that can replicate what you did to those plants?" he asked.

"Nope. Hopefully someone can hook me up though. Or I can

create one." I went through my mental catalogue. "I have a bunch of deadly potions, but none that sucks out the life of many living things at once." I shuddered, not even wanting to own such a potion. I didn't blame the Order for being wary.

"Your friends will help you."

I smiled slightly. He was right about that. I might be worried to death, but I had backup. They'd always be there for me. "I'll call them."

"Then let's get some rest."

He was right. The sun was already high in the sky, and we were burning our rest hours. Not to mention, the mood was officially killed. Chilly fear still raced over my arms.

"You can take my room," he said.

"I don't need to."

"I don't want to argue."

"Fine. Thank you."

We split then, not acknowledging the near-kiss.

As I walked by, he gripped my shoulder gently. "We'll fix this, Rowan."

His words made me feel a bit better, but he couldn't entirely drive the fear away. Nothing could do that. Not until they officially cleared me, and maybe not even then.

As I climbed the stairs, I called my sisters again, explaining what had happened with the potions.

"We'll get Lachlan right on it," Ana said. "And Hedy and Connor. Between the three of them, they can find something that will do the trick."

"Quick thinking, Rowan," Bree said. "There's all kinds of terrible potions that they don't monitor."

"No, they're only concerned with what *we* can do." I didn't understand why it was any different if I killed someone with a touch or if I did it with a potion bomb, but it probably had something to do with them thinking death-wielders were evil.

Which, fair enough. I could see why we might be creepy.

"Don't worry, Rowan," Bree said. "Even if you did get sent to the prison, we would find you. We'll *always* find you."

I nodded, smiling gratefully. Once I'd gotten away from the Rebel Gods, my sisters had bought me a tracking charm. They each had one, too. Had had them for years, actually, ever since my abduction. After losing me, they hadn't wanted to lose each other. With the charms, we could find each other anywhere in the world. It'd once saved Ana's life, in fact.

"Thanks, guys. Love you lots."

"Love you lots," they echoed.

I cut the connection with my sisters and stepped into the darkened bedroom. For some reason, it seemed bigger and darker. Emptier than before.

Lonelier.

It only made the fear worse. The worry.

I knew that a lot of it was caused by exhaustion, but knowing that didn't drive the worry away.

I sat on the bed, weighted down by it. Made cold by it.

A scratching noise sounded at the window, and I looked up.

Romeo sat there, along with Poppy and Eloise. Poppy had replaced her flower with a pretty orange leaf. A smile tugged at my face as I went to the window and opened it. The three little weirdos tumbled in.

I returned to the bed, and they jumped up to sit on the end.

You look sad. Romeo twisted his little hands together.

"Worried."

He nodded. *Yes. That's it. I'm not good with human feelings. Your faces are squashed and strange. Hard to read.*

"You do all right."

He gave me a fangy grin, then clambered up the blankets until he sat on my lap. Then he patted my hand with his smaller one. A tingle of warmth flowed through me.

"What are you doing?"

Making you feel better.

Poppy and Eloise trundled up and settled in by each hip.

"When was the last time you guys were in a dumpster?"

Poppy hissed her annoyance.

We've bathed. We're very clean, you know.

I nodded, a laugh bubbling out of me. "Of course. I bet Eloise makes you take regular baths."

The badger grumbled as if it were a difficult task.

"In between all her fighting, of course."

She grinned as if liking the sound of that.

Well, is it working? I smell nice, right? Romeo looked up at me, little nose pointed up toward my face.

"Yeah, actually." I wrapped my arms around him and cuddled my trash panda. Maybe it was weird, but I didn't care. And I chose to believe that they actually had taken baths. They were just like cats. Almost. "I have to go to a ball tomorrow. Do you think you guys could make me a dress?"

Romeo brightened, his head popping up from where he'd laid it on my shoulder. *Like Cinderella?*

"Exactly like Cinderella."

Of course *we can.*

Eloise grumbled. *Bad idea.*

I smiled and looked down at her. "Did you speak, Eloise?"

She just ignored me. But she was probably right. My Menacing Menagerie was better at fighting and dumpster diving. But as I fell asleep, I couldn't help but smile at the idea of them making me a dress. Probably out of whatever crap they found in a dumpster, but it'd be made with love, at least.

CHAPTER NINE

I woke to the sound of my sister's screeching.

"Rowan! Wake up!" Ana's voice carried up the stairs.

I popped upright, the Menacing Menagerie long gone. Probably off to menace some trash bins. Hopefully not the one in Maximus's kitchen.

With bleary eyes, I stumbled out of bed as Ana strode into the room. Her blonde hair was pulled up high, and she was dressed in an evening gown of royal blue.

I blinked. "What the heck?"

She twirled. "I'm going to a ball!"

Bree walked in behind her, dressed in siren red with her hair pulled back in a complicated twist. "Me too."

"And we'll kick ass and take names." Ana grinned dangerously and drew a sword from the ether, twirling it for effect.

"You're going with me tonight?"

"Not with you. Beside you. You're after the witches and the prize. We're backup to make sure they don't mess with the guests or any other innocents. We'll just blend in with the crowd and monitor. Jude's orders."

"Blend with the crowd?" My gaze scanned them. They

looked beautiful, but... "You guys still look like you're ready to throw down."

"That's because we're always ready to throw down. But those people don't know us. They'll just think we're awkward."

Awkward wasn't the word I'd use for them. They really did look beautiful. Insanely beautiful. Perfect dresses, makeup, hair, and all of that layered on top of kickass bodies. It was just that I also knew how deadly they were.

"You're right, I'm biased."

"Exactly." Ana waggled her brows. "And wait until you see Lachlan and Cade. Meeeow, can those two wear a tux."

Yeah, of course their boyfriends would look hot as hell in tuxes.

"I bet Maximus will clean up pretty nice." Bree gave an exaggerated leer.

I stifled a giggle, but couldn't hide the blush.

Ana's brows jumped. "Rowan! Spill."

"There's nothing to spill." Not yet, at least. I wanted to hold on to it for a little while longer. See if it went anywhere. "Why are you here?"

"To get you dressed!" Bree raised her arm, and only then did I notice the black bag slung over it. She held it out to me. "A dress for you."

"Maximus said he could have conjured one," Ana said. "But that it would have been ugly as a hound's backside. So we picked this out, and Hedy made a couple of modifications. You'll like them." She grinned knowingly.

I reached for the bag, my fingertips trembling just slightly.

We never dressed up, and to be honest, I didn't entirely hate the idea. Anticipation shivered through me as I unzipped the black plastic. Shimmering golden fabric fell out, waves upon waves of it.

"Oh my fates," I breathed. "It's beautiful"

It gleamed like gold, soft and silken, and I pulled it out. There was just so much of it.

"Wait!" Ana held out her hands. "You need to shower first."

I frowned, then sniffed myself. *Yep.* A shower was definitely in order. Quickly, excitement shivering through me, I hurried to the shower and jumped in. To my credit, I only thought about Maximus being naked in here twice.

Okay, maybe three times.

Four.

But I was clean and out in minutes. Ana and Bree stood in the doorway of the bathroom, oblivious to the idea of privacy.

"Hair first," Bree said.

"Is this a makeover?" I asked, suddenly nervous. "This seems like a makeover."

"Just going to polish you up some," Ana said. "You'll look fabulous."

"And wait until you see the special features on your dress," Bree said.

I nodded. It didn't take them long to do up my hair and makeup, though they wouldn't let me look in the mirror. When it finally came time for the dress, I was vibrating with anticipation.

It fit like a dream, smoothing down over my torso and falling in massive waves around my legs, all the way to the floor. Somehow, it was super light—I actually felt like I could run in it—but there was still a ton of fabric around my legs.

"It's a proper ball gown," I said.

Ana picked up a bag off a chair. My backup potion bomb bag. She plucked a bomb out of it and held it up, grinning. "And now it's time for the special features."

She dropped the bomb against my skirt, and it disappeared into a hidden pocket that was nestled amongst the waves of golden fabric. I couldn't feel the weight of it, but when I reached in, the bomb rose to my fingertips, as if propelled by magic.

My eyes widened, and I looked at Ana and Bree. "Oooh, a murder dress."

Ana and Bree grinned widely.

"It's been enchanted," Ana said. "You won't feel the weight of the potion bombs in the pockets, and they'll come to you easily when you reach your hand in."

"Wow." I took another bomb from her and dropped it in a pocket, then another. She was right. I couldn't feel them at all. "This is amazing."

I couldn't store potion bombs in the ether like I did with my sword because it was expensive and difficult to enchant an object that way. Sticking the electric sword in the ether had been worth the expense, but it was too difficult and pricey to do it with potion bombs that were one-time-use items.

But this dress...

"Holy fates, this thing is amazing." I'd filled all the pockets, and it still looked like a normal dress. No, scratch that. It looked like a fabulous dress.

I moved to the full-length mirror on the door and got my first good look. My jaw nearly dropped.

Yep. It was a fabulous dress. And I looked fabulous in it. Beautiful and mysterious and dangerous. My hair was swept back and my eyes done up in shimmery gray shadow.

Even better, I was deadly in this thing.

Bree stepped forward, my favorite flat-heeled black boots in her hands. "Even better, you can wear these with it. The skirt will cover them. And then you'll be ready to run for it when you need to."

Grinning, I took the boots. "Practical and comfortable."

As much as I admired high heels in shop windows, actually wearing them—especially on a job like this—was a death wish. I tugged on the boots and stood, swishing in front of the mirror. No matter how I moved, I couldn't see the boots.

"The dress is even supposed to be easy to run in," Bree said. "Ours are enchanted too. We tried and it's great."

Ana and Bree tugged up their ball gowns to show that they were also wearing boots. I smiled at them, pretty sure that this might be the best moment of my life.

"Thanks guys." I hugged them both.

"Got your back, sis," Ana said.

"Always," Bree added.

On the windowsill, the Menacing Menagerie sat, grinning widely. They might not have made the dress, but they seemed to like it. I waved at them, feeling a bit like Cinderella myself. Fortunately, their promise to make me a dress had been a joke.

My sisters and I climbed down the stairs to the main living area. I spotted Maximus first. Tall and handsome, he wore a perfectly fitted black tux. And holy fates, did he look *good.*

So good that I hardly even noticed Cade and Lachlan, who also looked pretty fantastic once I spotted them. I only had eyes for Maximus, though.

As soon as he saw me descending the stairs, he stopped.

His brows rose and his eyes flickered.

I glided toward him and stopped a few feet away.

"You look beautiful." His voice was rough.

I blushed, then wished I hadn't. Awkwardness made me step back. "So do you. Look good, I mean." *Oh my god, idiot.* "Ready to kick ass?"

He grinned. "Always."

Bree, Ana, Cade, and Lachlan took separate vehicles to the ball, while Maximus and I got into a big old limo that looked like a carefully preserved relic from a more glamorous era. The wisps swooped about as we climbed in.

"Wow." I slid in over the soft leather seat, marveling at how my dress moved so smoothly, never getting caught on anything and never tangling around my feet.

"I thought we'd do it up right." A sexy smile tugged at the corner of his mouth. "Not every day we go to a ball."

"I like how you think."

"And if we provide good entertainment for the Intermagic Games, the Order of the Magica may cut you a bit of slack."

I smiled. "I like how you think. It's all about perception, and even little things can twist someone's perspective."

"Exactly."

We rode along in silence for the rest of the way, each of us shooting an occasional glance at the other. Once in a while, I spotted white wisps through the window, keeping track of our progress for the viewing audience. I shifted, suddenly feeling awkward.

I was enjoying the adventure part of this whole thing—even the deadly bits—but I did not like being on TV. Or whatever the magical equivalent was.

By the time the limo pulled up outside of the palace, the sun had fully set. The driver opened the door, and Maximus helped me out. It was all for show, though. Not that he didn't have the manners, but I didn't need help. My dress almost helped *me* move. Never getting in the way, never a burden.

It was fantastic. Maybe my new thing would be fighting in ball gowns.

I grinned at the idea and took in the palace. It was *fantastic*. Situated right in the supernatural district of London, it rose five stories high, towers and turrets reaching toward the stars. It was a relic that had somehow survived the WWII bombing that had destroyed much of London. The white stone gleamed in the light, along with the pale gray tile on the roofs. Hundreds of windows glittered with lights from within. Swirling, colorful ball gowns passed by them.

Night-blooming roses lined the path up to the massive, sweeping front stairs, giving the place the most amazing scent. Fairy lights glittered in the trees—*real* fairy lights, since this was where magic could be out in the open—and gave the place a truly magical air.

Not just the magic that we all used day to day. But the fairy-tale magic that humans talked about. The romance and glitter and feeling that anything could happen.

I blinked, suddenly feeling like maybe *I* was actually Cinderella.

My gaze went to Maximus. My prince.

Heat rose in my cheeks. Not just because of Maximus, but because that thought was totally insane. I was here to kick ass and take names. To save the day. Just because I'd spent so much of my life locked up that I was now in a fantasy land over every little thing didn't mean that it was a good idea.

I shook the thought away and focused on the job at hand. My gaze snagged on four figures slipping through the grand doors. My sisters and their men. Good. They were here.

I searched the crowd then, my eyes widening slightly at the sheer number. When we'd first arrived, I'd only had eyes for the fairy-tale magic of this place.

Now?

Holy fates. Now, I was noticing all the dangerous supernaturals. Cinderella's prince sure had some iffy friends. There were supernaturals of all varieties—witches, fae, vampires, shifters, mages—and most of them were really freaking powerful. They wore their magic like they wore their finery. Out and loud. Signatures collided in the air, scents and sounds and feelings. Some of it was good, some of it bad.

All of it was strong.

I slowed my breathing and tried to get control of my magic.

No reason to flaunt it like these morons. They were like a bunch of freaking roosters, strutting around.

Maximus also kept his magic under wraps. He let the scent of cedar and the taste of whiskey run free, and I had to admit to enjoying it. But the rest of it, he hid.

He looked at me and held out an arm. I took it, unable to conceal the little grin of pleasure. I might be here to win, and stop the bad guys, but I was going to enjoy doing it.

Together, we made our way to the main steps, ascending in unison. As we entered the foyer, the white wisps flitted around our heads. No one seemed to notice or care. Or maybe they couldn't see them.

We entered the main ballroom at an upper balcony that encircled the entire dance floor, hovering twenty feet above the revelers. The arched ceiling overhead was painted with gold and hung with dozens of chandeliers. Instead of candles, more fairy lights flitted around the crystal and gold.

Between the sheer magical opulence and the dangerous nature of the partiers, it almost made my head spin.

"Do you have any idea what Cinderella looks like?" Maximus asked.

I shook my head. "Not really. Glass slippers, though. She'll be the only one wearing those."

We leaned over the balcony railing, searching below for a woman in glittering glass shoes. The dancers swept around each other, somehow all moving in unison in some kind of waltz or other old-fashioned dance. The band was made up of men and women wearing tall white wigs, curls piled high. Florian, the ghost librarian, would fit right in here.

"I don't see her," I said.

"Let's dance. Get a better view."

I nodded, my heart skipping a beat at the idea of dancing. We descended the wide staircase into the party below, and I felt like I was in a historical romance novel. I was all for this. Especially since I got to wear my boots and carry my potions.

When we reached the bottom, Maximus swept me into a spin that took my breath away. We twirled around the dance floor, not once stepping on each other's feet.

I laughed. "How did you learn to dance like this?"

"Movies. And dancing is a lot like fighting. At least, fighting well." He grinned, so devastatingly handsome that I couldn't look away.

And he had a point. Fighting well took grace and timing and skill.

I blinked, suddenly realizing that I *really* wasn't doing my job. How embarrassing would it be to lose the competition because I was distracted by a pretty dress and dancing? I shook my head slightly and began to search the crowd, my gaze dropping down to feet whenever I got a chance.

Skillfully, Maximus took us on a loop around the dance floor that twirled us by most of the other revelers, giving me a good view of many pairs of feet. We were near the edge when I thought I caught a flash of something sparkling and clear near the ground.

"Over there," I whispered. "Near the blonde woman and big man. He's definitely some kind of reptile shifter."

I couldn't see her face, not that it would necessarily tell me what kind of supernatural she was. But it might. The man obviously turned into something scaly, from the look of the slight green cast to his skin and the narrow pupils in his eyes.

Maximus expertly moved us into position near them, and I leaned over, trying to get a peek at her shoes. What Cinderella doing anyway, dancing with a snake shifter?

I was so preoccupied trying to get a look at her shoes that I lost the lead Maximus had created and bumped into the woman. She hissed and turned, her narrowed eyes as snakey and reptilian as her date's.

"What are you doing?" Her words were liberally coated in venom, and I was worried that she might spit some of the actual stuff at me.

"So sorry." I tried to pull away, but she leaned closer, clearly pissed.

"I'm enjoying my time here, and you just *bumped* into me?" Red started to combine with the green tinge to her skin, and I frowned.

Was she on something? She was more pissed than she should be.

"Why, I ought to—" She pulled her hand away from her date's and raised it, claws glinting in the light.

"Jeez, lady, chill out." The last thing I needed was a scene with some nut job on party drugs.

She hissed again.

Yep, this was going south fast, and for no apparent reason. Except that it made for good viewing, and maybe she was a plant on behalf of the Intermagic Games. It'd be pretty damned hard to get Cinderella's slipper if I was kicked out of the ball.

Quickly, I shoved my hand into one of my dress pockets, hoping I'd chosen the right one. When the little spray bottle rose to meet my fingertips, I grinned and gripped it.

"What are you smiling about?" She leaned close, her eyes crazy.

I yanked the bottle out of my pocket and sprayed her in the face with an opalescent liquid.

Her eyes fluttered half closed, and she smiled as her gaze fogged over.

I turned back to Maximus. "Let's go."

"Hey! What'd you do to my date?" The snake man's voice followed us as we drifted away.

I leaned back and spritzed him, too, watching as his eyes drifted down and his lips turned up in a happy, vacant smile.

Maximus twirled us away, dancing expertly through the crowd. My heartbeat began to slow as we put distance between us and the crazy serpent shifters. Mini crisis averted.

"What did you do to them?" Maximus asked.

"Forgetfulness potion. A bit like what we used on the guard in Switzerland, but in aerosol form. It'll only last a few minutes, but she won't remember us. Neither will her date."

"Good thinking. Getting kicked out would slow us down."

"My thoughts exactly." I searched the crowd, spotting my sisters positioned on either side of the room, their gazes sweeping the crowd, looking for the witches. "Let's do one more circuit, then search smaller rooms."

We didn't find Cinderella or any of our competitors on our last turn around the dance floor, though I did enjoy it. By the time we stopped, my cheeks were flushed and my breathing quick.

"There's a lot more space in this palace," Maximus said. "They could have snuck off to another room, or perhaps be on the grounds."

Just the idea of how much space there was left to cover made me cringe. I looked up at the balcony, turning to inspect the whole thing. On the far side, I caught sight of another flash of clear crystal near the ground. A woman's shoe as she stepped away from the railing.

"Come on!" I grabbed Maximus's hand and pulled him to the stairs.

"Not so fast," he murmured.

I slowed, just a bit, taking it down a notch from an all-out run. He had a point. Part of this challenge was not getting kicked out, and pushing people aside as you sprinted through the crowd was definitely bad form.

We made our way up the stairs as quickly as we could, then over to the room where the woman must have gone. A fancy sign indicated that there were refreshments inside.

Maximus and I ducked inside a fairly large room that was dotted with couches and lined by bookshelves. Food tables lined the edges of the walls. By the time I reached the center of the room, it was clear that something was up.

Fist, the lady with the shoes wasn't here.

There were four figures, though, scattered around the edges of the room but ignoring the tables full of canapés and champagne. They turned to face me.

Two fae and two shifters.

The door clicked shut behind us, and a lock turned.

"Well, crap." I looked at Maximus. "These morons are ambushing us."

CHAPTER TEN

The two shifters growled in unison. In their human forms, they looked like big, brown-haired bruisers, their noses bashed from long-ago fights and their shoulders broad enough to threaten the seams of their poorly fitting tux jackets. The fae were elegant and sophisticated in matching black formal wear. They looked at us like we were bugs, their blue wings glittering in the fairy lights.

The only two who weren't here were the illusionists, and I wasn't going to assume that. They could hide themselves, after all. Without a doubt, they were our scariest competitors.

"So, you're ganging up because we won the last round, huh?" I taunted.

"Just for a while," Imani, the female fae, said. She was beautiful, with dark skin and long braids. Her magic vibrated out from her, feeling like a rush of cool silk against my skin. "We'll turn on them next." She nodded at the wolves. "But they expect that."

It was fair enough, but I preferred an all-out race to the end rather than these sneaky machinations.

I reached into the pockets of my skirts, drawing two potion

bombs. Maximus drew a sword and shield from the ether. No way I'd go with a blade—not if I wanted to keep my lovely dress blood free. I didn't want to hurt them too badly.

The shifters growled low in their throats as their magic swirled around them. They shifted into their wolf form, two large beasts with long fangs and even longer claws. Their growls made the hair on my arms stand up.

"I'll take them," Maximus muttered.

"I've got the fae." I darted right as one threw a blast of glittery blue magic at me. It pricked against my skin as I dived, barely managing to avoid it.

I had no idea what was in that blue cloud, but I was pretty sure I didn't want to figure it out. Fortunately, I was able to move quickly in my enchanted dress, darting behind a huge wingback chair. I peeked around and hurled my first bomb at the male fae. Jabari, I thought his name was.

He was fast, though, darting right and avoiding my bomb by inches.

I scowled. At this range, I should have at *least* hit his shoulder. Concentrating, I threw another, aiming right for the middle of the female fae. Imani was just as fast as her friend, darting away right before it collided with her.

But that was wrong, too. Given her speed and my close proximity to her, I *should* have hit her arm.

I sniffed the air, trying to get a hint of the illusionists' signature. I smelled nothing. Felt nothing. Taste was a big fat negative, as well. If they were here, they were keeping things under wraps, using minimal magic and hiding their signatures.

It was enough to give our opponents the advantage though. Maximus was fighting like a madman—a skilled one—but he couldn't land a solid blow on the wolves. I'd seen them in action during the opening ceremonies. They'd been giving it their all and they were fast, but not as fast as Maximus.

I frowned and turned my attention back to the fae, reaching for more bombs. Before I could throw one, Imani hurled a blast of pink magic at the chair. The thing exploded, sending cushions and wood flying everywhere.

I dived away and skidded to a stop under a table covered in hors d'oeuvres. "The hosts aren't going to like that!"

She just hissed, and I knew she had to be powering up another blast.

But wait—hadn't there been a punch bowl on top of this table?

Oh, shit.

If there was punch up there—and I was pretty sure there was —I'd be a mess if this table exploded. Not to mention the canapés. I needed this disguise to fit into the ball. And I looked damned good in it.

Fast as I could, I crawled out from under the table, making it to the safety of the corner of the room just before the table went boom. Punch flew into the air, red and bright and sparkling. It splattered the silk wallpaper and I winced.

"You are the worst guests!" I threw my potion bomb at the fae, this time aiming slightly right of her. It was a guess, but I guessed right.

She darted right, directly into my line of fire.

"Ha!" I couldn't help but gloat, even though my mother would have said it wasn't flattering.

But I was definitely right—the illusionists were in here. No question. They were changing the scene just slightly. Making me see my opponents not where they truly were, but about a foot off. Same for Maximus. No way he would keep missing the wolves.

I dug into my dress pocket to find the potion that would break the illusion—I only had a couple, so I needed to be sparing—but Jabari threw a blue glitter blast at me.

I darted away, hand still in my pocket.

Too slow.

The cloud hit me in the arm, and my limb went entirely numb. *Oh, crap.*

I tried to move it, but nothing.

Double crap.

I couldn't let their paralyzing glitter bomb hit me in the chest again, that was for damned sure. I'd be out like a light. Maybe permanently.

This was just a game. Not worth *death.*

I reached into my pocket with my good arm. Thank fates I'd trained with both. My fingertips closed around the star-shaped glass bottle, and I yanked it free and threw it to the ground in front of me.

It broke open, sparkly pink lights flying out and zipping around the room.

A moment later, two pale figures were revealed, standing by the door. White hair and white eyes matched their ivory dresses. The fae and the wolves wobbled in their positions briefly, finally standing still in a spot about a foot from where they had been. Before I could say a word or throw a potion bomb at the illusionists, they were gone, darting right out the door, their dresses fluttering behind them.

"Cowards," Jabari spat.

"Duh." My tone was scathing. "And so are you, ganging up on us like this." I hiked a thumb at the door through which the fae had disappeared. "They're going to try to beat you to the clue now."

"Then we'll have to be fast." He raised his hands, and his magic flared.

Poor bastard. I darted away before he could blast me, then hurled a stunner at him. It crashed right against his chest, splashing blue liquid over him.

His eyes widened just briefly, then he tumbled over. He'd be out for a good few minutes.

"Not so fast *now*." I grinned and dug into my pocket for another stunner.

But Imani was faster. She avoided my first bomb—which was a little off since it was my left arm—and managed to throw one of those miserable blue glitter clouds at me.

I dived out of the way just in time, but it flew through the door into the hallway outside.

Oh fates!

That wasn't good.

Nor was the short yelp that followed after. I rolled over to glare at the fae, who seemed temporarily surprised. I used it to my advantage, hitting her in the chest with a stunner. She toppled over a second later.

On the other side of the room, Maximus was slicing at the wolves with his sword. Though they were fast, he was faster, delivering wound after wound. They were small, since I thought he was keen not to actually kill them, but it was enough to drive them off. With the fae out, the wolves turned and darted, leaving droplets of blood behind as they sprinted from the room.

They were off to find the glass slipper, and we needed to hurry.

Somehow, Maximus had managed to avoid every splash of blood, which was impressive. I'd seen his quick moves before, but they'd never come in handier.

"Someone got hit in the hall." I turned and hurried out, moving as quickly as I could so as not to be spotted.

A butler lay on the ground, frozen in his sharp black suit. Crap.

Maximus appeared at my side, immediately spotting the problem. He bent to inspect the man.

My arm, which had previously been frozen, was starting to

get some feeling back. Thank fates it was temporary.

"Are you all right?" Maximus asked.

"My legs!" Panic echoed in the butler's voice.

"They'll be fine." I dropped to my knees next to him, flapping my partially useless arm. "I was hit in the arm a few minutes before you, and I'm already getting feeling back."

His eyes latched onto mine like I was a lifeline, and I nodded, trying to reassure him. He seemed to believe me, thank fates. I didn't want to leave him here, afraid, but I also didn't want to waste any time.

The fae sprinted out of the room while we knelt on the floor with the butler, ignoring us now. They'd shaken off the effects of my stunners quickly, and I hoped they got hopelessly lost in some kind of hedge maze in the back garden.

"Let me get you onto a sofa," Maximus said.

The butler nodded, and Maximus lifted him like he was nothing. We re-entered the partially destroyed room, and the butler moaned like he'd been shot.

I frowned guiltily at the mess I'd helped create, then spotted Romeo, Poppy, and Eloise sitting amongst the scattered, destroyed food, massive grins on their faces. They were completely ignoring the food that sat on the undamaged tables.

Romeo held up a smooshed eclair. *Fantastic!*

I eyed him. "Sweet little weirdo."

He just grinned.

"Can you guys sit with our friend here until he feels better?" I asked. "Maybe get him a snack."

"Who are they?" The butler looked at the animals, wide-eyed.

"Buddies of mine. Really nice. Freshly bathed, I promise."

Poppy hissed, as if offended.

I shot her an apologetic glance. "Sorry, Poppy." I looked back at the butler. "Would it be all right if we left you with them? The jerks who hit you with that stunning cloud are after something we want, and we need to beat them to it."

The butler's eyes lit up. "Oh! You're part of the competition! Yes, yes, go get them!"

"Any idea where Cinderella is?" I asked.

He frowned.

"Are you not allowed to aid the contestants?" I asked.

"No, no. It's not that. I was just thinking." He smiled, conspiratorially. "Actually, it is up to us if we wish to help with clues. All of the staff, I mean. And since you helped me, I'll help you."

"Oh, thanks." I'd have helped him anyway, obviously. I didn't really want to live in a world where I jumped over fallen old men and just kept going.

"Cinderella and the prince are in the back gardens. Behind the house, down the long corridor." He waggled his brows. "I think it's getting serious."

"Thank you. So much." I grinned at him.

Romeo hopped up on the couch next to him and handed him a non-squished eclair, then glanced at me. *I assumed he wanted a boring, non-smooshed human version.*

"I think you guessed right." I grinned. "Take care of my new friend."

The three little animals saluted, and I thanked my lucky stars for my weird sidekicks.

Maximus and I thanked the butler again, then ran for it, sprinting down the long balcony and toward the smaller set of stairs back there. Since Cinderella was technically outside of the ball, I was less worried about getting caught. Not to mention the fact that everyone else had a lead on us. They might not know where old Cindy was hanging out, but that didn't mean they wouldn't get lucky.

We raced down the stairs, quickly finding the large hallway that led to the back gardens. It was empty, the walls decorated with fancy paintings. Chandeliers hung every twenty feet, sending a warm glow glittering over the space. Our footsteps were quiet on the lush carpet underfoot, and I pressed my fingers to my comms charm as I ran.

"Bree? Ana?" I whispered. "Any sight of your friend?"

We'd agreed not to use words like "target" and "prey" in case people were listening in on their comms charms. That was the problem with crowded spaces like this. I also didn't need the wisps overhearing. They were trailing behind, desperately trying to keep up.

"None," Bree whispered. "We're checking smaller rooms now."

"We're headed to the back gardens to find Cindy," I whispered.

"Good luck," Ana and Bree said in low voices.

I cut the connection and picked up the pace. We exited the huge hall onto an outdoor walkway. It was just as wide as the interior hall had been, bordered on either side by ornate white pillars. The moon gleamed on the marble underfoot, and the rich scent of roses filled the air. The sound of splashing fountains completed the scene, but it was the two women up ahead that really caught my eyes.

Each had long blonde hair, and they stomped forward with determination.

Hang on...

Didn't Cinderella have mean, jealous stepsisters who treated her like a slave?

"Hey!" I shouted, hurrying up from behind.

Maximus gave me a curious look, but I ignored him.

The two stopped and turned. Neither was very pretty, and it wasn't so much a product of their features or figures. It was more the scowl on their faces. Anyone with a scowl like that would end up looking like a miserable old witch.

"Are you Cinderella's stepsisters?" I asked as I approached, my skirts swishing around my ankles.

The one on the right raised her blonde brows. "What of it?"

That meant yes, I thought. "Well, it seems like you're headed off to break up her party with Prince Charming."

They both shrugged.

"That's a dick move," I said, ignoring Maximus's gaze. I wasn't sure if he knew the story of Cinderella, but that chick deserved a break. "You're hoping she'll be your slave forever, so you don't want her going off with the prince. Or having a good time at all."

They both hissed. I was getting close enough now to really make out their features, and there was something a bit off about them.

"It's her job!" the sister on the left hissed.

I frowned. The voice was weird. And the eyes...

Now that I was close enough to see them, their eyes were purple.

Two sisters. Two witches.

Only they weren't Cinderella's sisters at all. They were the evil witches, here to scoop us on the clue. Somehow, they'd glamoured themselves to look like Cinderella's bitchy stepsisters.

Quickly, I pressed my fingertips to my comms charm. "Found your friends. Back gardens, on the big walkway."

"On it," Bree whispered.

"What's that?" the witch demanded.

Clearly she still thought her disguise was working. They'd changed their hair and faces. Even their shapes. They were shorter and curvier now. But their eyes—they couldn't hide those. I didn't know what the hell these two were or what they wanted in the long run, but I knew I didn't want them to have it. And it'd be better if I killed time till my backup was here. I just had to hope that the other competitors hadn't beaten us to the back garden.

I glanced at Maximus, and he didn't seem to get what was going on. I'd never told him about the purple eyes, I realized.

"Well, we'll just be on our way," the witch said.

Ah, that was interesting. They'd been super invested in killing me before. Now, they'd just let me go?

In exchange for the Truth Teller, it seemed.

"I don't think so," I said. "Even if you were Cindy's evil sisters, I wouldn't let you go screw up her date."

At that moment, I vowed to myself I'd get the clue without ruining her chances with the prince.

Something dark rose up within the witch on the right. I could see it in her eyes, as if tar were boiling behind them, rising up and filling her.

The one on the left tried to keep it together. "You cannot command us!"

"Sure I can." I grinned, winking at the angry witch.

Boy, was she pissed.

And from the look of the dark magic that roiled out from her, starting at her feet like a black cloud and bubbling over the tile, she was *dangerous*.

I didn't know what magic she possessed, but suddenly, prickles of fear snaked over my skin.

Footsteps sounded from behind us, and I glanced back, hope welling in my chest.

Satisfaction shot through me.

Backup had arrived!

Ana, Bree, Lachlan, and Cade sprinted toward us, weapons drawn.

I turned back, just in time to see the women shift into their enormous bird forms. Like monstrous owls, their eyes glinted and their beaks snapped. The angry one lunged for me, then pulled back, shrieking in pain.

"Ha!" The binding charm was still clearly working. They could do no damage with beaks or claws.

The birds hissed, then launched themselves into the sky. Powerful wings carried them upwards.

From behind, my friends skidded to a halt.

"I've got this," Bree said as her magic flared.

"Be careful, at least," Cade said.

I turned. Her silver Valkyrie wings flared behind her. Ana had shifted into her large black crow form, and was already pushing off the ground and swooping into the air.

"I'm just tracking them." Bree launched herself after Ana, flying close behind.

"We'll follow from the ground," Cade said.

Lachlan nodded.

"I'm out." I saluted Cade and Lachlan, then turned and sprinted off, Maximus at my side.

We needed to figure out what the hell those evil witches were, but for now, I needed to find Cindy. We had to get that clue. *And* we had to keep the others from ruining her chances with the prince. I tried to keep my footsteps quiet as we ran, and a few moments later, the pathway spilled out into a massive patio that overlooked the moonlit garden.

It was beautiful.

And right in the middle, Cindy and the prince sat on a bench. Her sparkling pink skirts trailed over the ground, making her look like a beautiful flower. Her head was tilted toward the prince. Knees too.

My amateur body-language reading indicated that she was digging him. Big time.

No way I'd screw that up for her. Not when the alternative was a lifetime spent scrubbing her bitchy stepsisters' house.

I skidded to a halt, grabbing Maximus's arm and pulling him behind a huge planter full of giant green ferns. I tucked myself back in the shadows, panting as quietly as I could while I tried to catch my breath.

"Why are we stopping?" he whispered. "She's right there."

"We can't just charge up and demand her shoe! This is her big moment. She's meeting the love of her life."

He frowned and turned, looking at the scene. Then his gaze met mine. "So, what do we do?"

I looked around, frantic. In the distance, I spotted a beautiful clock tower. It was just moments before midnight. A minute, maybe two.

"We wait." I peered around the planter to look at Cindy. "She's going to run for it when the clock strikes midnight. We'll follow her and try not to screw with her shoe too much."

"Wait, what?" Maximus's brow furrowed.

"You must not be familiar with the story."

He shook his head.

"We need to get the clue in the shoe, but we can't take it. The prince has to find it. It's how he'll locate her later."

"With her shoe?" He looked disbelieving.

"I'll explain it all later." I turned back to look down the pathway, praying that our competitors weren't behind us. They'd blow this thing out of the water.

I didn't know if there were other shoes with clues for them to find, like there had been multiple maps. But *this* Cindy was my Cindy, and I wasn't going to let anyone mess with her.

My gaze darted back and forth between Cindy and the pathway, my heart lodged in my throat as I waited to see if this situation would get a whole lot more complicated.

"Come on, Cindy, come on," I muttered, turning back to check out the path one more time.

The wolves careened onto it, this time dressed in their tuxes as humans.

My stomach dropped. "Shit."

Maximus turned back to look, then his eyes darted to mine. "I'll hold them off."

I looked at the clock. There were just seconds left. I nodded. "I need at least a few minutes. I'll meet you on the main stairs out front."

He nodded, then took off, sprinting down the path toward the wolves. I looked back at Cindy just as the clock tolled midnight.

CHAPTER ELEVEN

Cinderella's brows rose in shock, and she gasped, shooting a look of horror at the clock. She turned back and said something to the prince, but I couldn't hear what it was. Then she was gone, sprinting off.

The prince stood there, dumbfounded. He'd go after her soon, once he got over his shock. But I needed just a few seconds alone with Cindy and her shoe.

I raced toward the prince, drawing a potion out of my pocket. I squinted at it in the dim moonlight, making sure I chose the right one. No way I wanted to hit him with something deadly. Not even a long-acting stunner.

The purple bottle gleamed back at me. Yep, this would work. It'd only stun him for a minute, maybe two. He heard me approaching and turned, surprise on his face. I threw the glass bomb at his feet, and it exploded, purple dust flying upward.

He blinked and sneezed, then stood stock-still.

I grinned and ran past. "I'll make sure you get the shoe."

Then I was gone, racing after Cindy. She wasn't far ahead of me. Unlike myself, she wore heels. *Glass* heels. Dummy.

I reached her as she tore down the main front steps in front of the palace. No one was here anymore, not even a lonely butler or guard. Probably scavenging in the kitchens. At least, that was what I'd be doing if I were staff at a big party like this.

Cindy rushed down the stairs, pink skirts swishing and glittering under the fairy lights. She didn't trip like I expected her to, however. Instead, she got halfway down the stairs, tugged off her right shoe, and dropped it on the step. She spared it one last glance and ran for it, leaving it behind in the moonlight.

Cindy left bait for the prince.

Clever Cindy.

I sprinted down after it and swept it up.

"Hey!" Her shout sounded through the night air.

I looked at her. "I'll make sure the prince gets it. I promise."

She studied me hard. "How did you know?"

I shrugged and grinned. "Fairy godmother."

Okay, it was a lie. But it was fun and she bought it and damned if I wouldn't get it to the prince.

She nodded, then ran for it, shouting her thanks over her shoulder. A carriage waited for her—an honest-to-god carriage pulled by horses—and she clambered up inside.

I turned my attention to the shoe, inspecting it. Tied to a tiny loop of glass on the back of the heel was a little scroll of paper. I pulled it off and opened it, worried that I'd find her phone number for the prince.

Instead, it was decorated with the crest of the Intermagic Games. I wasn't sure if Cindy had known this was here or if it was magic, but damned if it wasn't cool.

The little white wisps floated around my head, and I couldn't help but grin. There might be deadly stakes in this game—not just my murderous competitors and the deadly challenges, but the evil witches—but it was kinda fun.

I tucked the little paper into my bra and turned just in time to see the prince race down the stairs after me. His perfect brown hair was windblown and his eyes panicked.

"Did you see her?" he demanded.

I nodded immediately, holding out the shoe. "She dropped this. Maybe you can use it to find her."

He frowned and took it. "Her shoe?"

"It will fit only her." I grinned. "So you should like, search the whole country and find her."

It was a ridiculous idea, but he nodded, delighted.

I grinned. Mission accomplished.

Except for my dastardly opponents.

"You need to get out of here, though. Now." I shooed the prince. "Dangerous people are coming."

"To my ball?" He stiffened. "Why, I won't stand for that!"

Oh, dang. That had been the wrong thing to say.

At the same moment, the fae sprinted toward the top of the stairs, panting. Their black formal wear was rumpled and their eyes annoyed. The illusionists followed behind, each wearing an identical white sheath dress. Their gazes riveted to the prince.

"Hide the shoe!" I hissed. "That's what they want."

They had no idea that I'd taken the clue from it.

But the prince was too slow. The damned shoe glittered in the moonlight like a beacon.

"I've got the clue!" I shouted. "It's not in the shoe anymore."

The two fae sneered at me.

"I trust you as far as I can throw you," Imani hissed.

"What's going on?" the prince demanded.

"You're just caught in the middle of something," I said. "But you need to hang on to that shoe. Do *not* let it go."

"I *know* that." He tucked the shoe into an inner pocket on his coat, then drew a sword and shield from the ether.

I gave him an appraising look. "Not bad, Prince."

"How do you think I keep my kingdom safe?"

Honestly, I had no idea if he was even a real person or a fairy-tale figment of the Intermagic Games, so I just smiled.

Together, we turned to face our opponents. The four of them sneered, then charged.

They raced down the stairs, both of the fae winding up their magic. It swelled in the air, growing stronger as they ran. The illusionists raised their hands as well, ready to scare the shit out of us, probably.

I dug into my pocket and pulled out the last of my illusion-breaking potions, then hurled it into the stairs that rose up in front of us. The pink lights swirled up, and the illusionists hissed. Clearly, they could feel the dampening power on their magic.

"Fine!" hissed the one on the left. "We'll do it the violent way." She drew a sword from a sheath at her back, and charged.

Before she could reach us, the fae threw their glittery blue stunner clouds. The prince charged the clouds, and I shouted.

He ignored me, slamming his shield into the poofs of dust. Magic reverberated from the metal, and the clouds bounced off the shield, flying back toward the fae. The sparkly blue stuff hit Jabari right in the chest, and he collapsed backward.

Wow. "What is *in* that shield?"

It had slammed a cloud backward. Insane.

"Magic, obviously." The prince charged the illusionist who held the sword, and they clashed in a battle of ringing metal and grunts.

Maximus appeared at the top of the stairs a moment later, looking disheveled. One stripe of red blood marred his flawless white dress shirt, but it didn't look like his, since the shirt wasn't torn. Clearly, the wolves were taken care of.

He eyed the scene, absorbing it quickly. Then he grinned and raised his hands. His magic swelled on the air, bringing with it the scent of cedar and the taste of whiskey.

No one seemed to notice, though, and a moment later, dozens of glass slippers spilled from his hands. They toppled down the stairs, some shattering and others staying intact.

Imani, who had been about to attack, turned, her eyes wide. She hadn't seen Maximus conjure the shoes, and in the heat of battle, didn't seem to remember that was a skill of his.

She charged up the stairs to grab a shoe. One of the illusionists followed, yanking up her narrow dress and sprinting.

The prince kept up the attack on the illusionist with the sword, finally driving her to the ground on her knees.

"Fine, fine!" she begged. "I quit!"

The prince stepped back, panting. He kept his sword and shield raised—he was no dummy—then nodded to the shoes that scattered the top of the stairs. "I think you're after those."

She surged upright and spit at his feet, then turned and raced up the stairs. Maximus hurried down, avoiding them. Any second now they would figure out our ruse.

The prince turned to me.

"You'd better get out of here," I said. "They're going to want the real thing soon, and you need it."

He nodded. "Indeed I do. Godspeed to you, danger woman."

"Danger woman?" I grinned, liking that, but he was already turning and striding off.

Maximus joined me. "Did you get it?"

"I got it. Now, let's vamoose. They're going to be real pissed when they figure out those aren't the actual clues."

I looked up. Both fae were scowling.. I turned and hurried down the stairs, Maximus at my side.

"That was my first ball, and I'd say it was a success." I grinned up at him.

"Likewise." He frowned. "They will find clues eventually, though. Otherwise, the game can't continue."

I nodded. He was right. "Then we'd better hurry." We

reached the bottom of the stairs, and I searched for the limo we'd taken to get here. "Where's our ride?"

"I can call it."

I looked around, suddenly thirsty and ravenous. Across the massive, beautiful lawn, there was a street, and across from that, there was a little pub. No one would look for us there. Not so close to the ball.

I grabbed Maximus's hand. "Come on." I pulled him across the lawn. As we walked, I pressed my fingertips to my comms charm. "Ana, Bree? How's it going?"

"Lost the target," Bree said. "Flew over the city, into the human part. Couldn't keep going."

Damn. But it was a smart move. No one needed the humans seeing a winged woman or a crow the size of a Volkswagen. "You out of the ball?"

They must be, if Bree was using words like target.

"We are," Ana said.

"Meet us at the Prophecy and Pint. It's a pub across from the palace's front lawn."

"On it."

By the time we got to the sidewalk in front of the Prophecy and Pint, Ana and Bree were there. They must have flown over. We stopped in front of them.

"You okay?" Bree asked.

"Fine. We got the clue."

Maximus took off his suit coat and tossed it in the trash. It had been slashed to bits by the wolves' claws, anyway. He rolled up his sleeves, looking dashing as hell.

Suddenly, the dress was too long for me. Too much.

I'd had a good time—a fabulous time, really—but I wanted to get back to myself. At least a bit.

A pair of discarded scissors peeked out of the trash can, glinting under the street lamp.

It was a sign.

I reached for them and began cutting off my skirt at mid thigh.

"What are you doing?" Ana asked.

"Making it a little more punk rock." With my tall black boots and the gold dress with a short poofy skirt, I looked pretty damned cool. And there were even a few pockets at the top, filled with potions.

Maximus's magic flared, and he conjured a short black leather coat. He handed it to me. I put it on, then shook out my hair.

"Badass," Bree said. "Let's go get a drink."

I shoved the discarded gold silk deep into the trash can so that no one would see it, then followed Bree, Ana, and Maximus into the pub. Cade and Lachlan were already waiting at a table in the corner. The pub was quiet and small, with a few crowded tables and a sleepy-looking bartender.

We picked up some pints from the bar and placed an order for late-night food, then headed to the table where Cade and Lachlan sat, a pint in front of each of them.

"How'd you get here so fast?" I asked.

"Bree told us where to go, and Lachlan transported us." Cade smiled.

Lachlan stood and polished off his beer. "Speaking of, I need to get back to the Protectorate. Hedy and Connor are working on the potion to fool the Order of the Magica about your magic, and I promised I'd come back and help."

Gratitude tightened my throat. "Thank you."

He nodded like it was nothing, then pressed a quick kiss to Ana's lips and left.

I took a steadying sip of my drink, grateful for my friends, and looked at everyone.

"Did you find your clue?" Cade asked.

I reached into my bodice and pulled out the tiny piece of paper. "Yep." The paper was stiffly curled, and I unrolled it, then read, "Three p.m., tomorrow night." I looked up. "I think it's a ticket."

"For what?" Maximus asked.

"It doesn't say. Just says to meet in the city of Dubrovnik at three p.m. Good for two passengers to the final confrontation."

"That means this is almost over," Maximus said.

I nodded. "I think so."

Bree frowned. "Dubrovnik is in Croatia. On the coast."

"So it could be a boat," Maximus said.

"If you got that clue first, I'd bet good money that your time of departure is slightly ahead of the others," Ana said. "The lead is your reward."

"Let's hope we don't lose it, then." I looked up as the barman appeared, balancing a few plates.

He frowned. "Can't say it'll be any good. Had to heat it up in the microwave."

I grinned and took the plates of steak and stilton pie. "Thanks. It'll be great."

And it was. We'd ordered enough for the table—just the leftovers from the day's menu—and we ate silently and ravenously for a few minutes.

When I was done, I looked up, catching sight of the wisps entering through the main door. "They've found us."

"Doesn't take the little bastards long, does it?" Maximus said. "I'll be glad to see the end of them."

I nodded. It was time to get going. I looked at Maximus. I wanted to stay with him, but he was a distraction. Not only did I need my sleep for tomorrow, but I had things to deal with. "I'm going to head back and sleep at my place. I want to check on Hedy and Lachlan's...ah, check on them."

I tried not to stare directly at the wisps, but it was hard.

Maximus looked like he wanted to say something, but he just nodded. "I'll see you tomorrow."

We split up, heading our own ways. Maximus left for his house in London, I assumed, while the rest of us used a transport charm to get back to the Protectorate.

The night was chilly in Scotland as we arrived on the front lawn. The wisps hadn't followed us, and I was certain they wouldn't be able to make it past the Protectorate's border.

I turned to face Hedy's tower, catching sight of the Cats of Catastrophe chasing the Pugs of Destruction across the wide, moonlit lawn. What they would do with them if they caught them, I had no idea.

I looked at my sisters and Cade. "Thanks for coming tonight."

"I'm just sorry we couldn't catch those damn witches," Ana said.

"We're going to have to go debrief Jude," Bree said. "They definitely want the final prize, and somehow they're clued into where the challenges are happening."

I nodded, sharing her assessment. "I'm going to go check with Hedy, Connor, and Lachlan. I want to see if there's any way I can help."

Bree reached out and squeezed my arm. "Try not to worry. We're going to get the Order of the Magica off your back. Promise."

Ana hugged me. "We wouldn't let them take you."

"That would mean going on the run." My stomach felt hollow just at the idea. "I don't want to leave you."

"We'd go with you, dummy." Bree gave me a look that said I was a moron for thinking otherwise, and Ana nodded her head vigorously.

My eyes smarted with tears. "I couldn't let you do that."

"Don't care," Ana said.

"And it won't matter," Bree added. "We'll find a way out of this. It's hardly the worst thing we've faced."

They were right. There were plenty of times the three of us had faced certain death and managed to weasel our way out. While a lifetime sentence at the Prison for Magical Miscreants sounded bad, there was worse.

I said goodnight, then headed across the lawn to Hedy's lonely tower. It sat near the edge of the property, away from the main castles. "In case I blow the place to hell," Hedy had once said.

It wasn't a bad idea.

Warm yellow lights glowed welcomingly from the windows as I approached, but the atmosphere inside the tower was far different.

Tension creased the brows of the three occupants. Connor, Hedy, and Lachlan all looked harried and tired as they bent over tables full of ingredients and herbs, vials and little metal tools. Hedy was wearing one of her usual flowy dresses, but it looked wrinkled and rough. Her lavender hair was pulled up on her head, a messy knot that spoke volumes about how hard she'd been working. Connor's flop of dark hair was also a rat's nest, and there was a coffee stain on his band T-shirt. The Proclaimers, this time. Lachlan hadn't changed out of his tux, just shed the jacket and rolled up his sleeves.

They were working so hard to help me. Damn, I was lucky to have them.

"How's it going?" I asked, my nerves a tight ball in my throat.

The three of them looked up, startled. They'd been so engrossed in their work that they hadn't seemed to notice me enter.

"Fine," Hedy said, but I could hear the lie in her voice.

"Smashing," Connor croaked.

"Not as well as when I left to attend the ball." Lachlan told the truth, at least.

Hedy smacked him. "We didn't anticipate the ingredients would decay when they came in contact with each other."

"We thought we had it." Connor frowned. "We didn't."

I approached, staring at the ingredients scattered across the table. "What's the main issue?"

Connor gestured to a large mirror sitting on top of the heavy wooden table, propped against the wall. On it, a semi-hazy image of the field of pumpkins showed. It looked a bit like a weird movie, and I watched as the vines withered.

"That's how people watch the Intermagic Games?" I asked. In all the stress of the competitions, I hadn't had a chance to figure it out. Staying alive had been more interesting.

"It is," Hedy said. "Just a simple spell that you place on your mirror, and you're hooked into the competition."

My stomach dropped a bit. "So *everyone* is watching."

"Any supernatural with a mirror can watch, yes," Hedy said.

"Damn." The idea stressed me out even more.

"The issue is that we're trying to replicate the rate of decay on the plants," Connor said. "Trying to make something that looks exactly like what you did. So the Order can't question you at all."

I nodded, seeing the problem. "Can I help?"

"You probably could," Hedy said. "But right now, you need to rest. Isn't there another competition coming up soon?"

"The final challenge. Tomorrow."

She nodded. "That's the one. You need to survive that first. The final challenge is always the most difficult. That's your priority."

"But if we don't figure this out, I'll be tossed in prison."

"I know." She flattened her face into a calming expression, and it kind of worked on me. "But you need to survive the fight first. Get some sleep. If there's time later to help, come on down. But for now, we've got it under control."

"We promise." Connor squeezed my arm.

"Thank you." I tried to put every bit of gratitude that I could into my voice.

"'Course." Hedy grinned. "Now go. You have to sleep so you can kick arse tomorrow, and we have to work."

I saluted and left, hurrying across the lawn. The moon was high in the sky, gleaming on the mountains that surrounded the castle. The castle looked enchanted on nights like this.

I couldn't help but think of Maximus as I climbed the stairs to my apartment. Memories of the last couple of days flashed in my mind's eye, along with longing. He haunted me as I walked down the quiet corridor.

When I saw him standing outside my door, I stopped and blinked.

CHAPTER TWELVE

"What are you doing here?" I asked, dumbfounded.

He turned to face me. "I forgot that I had something to say."

"Yeah?" I approached slowly, then stopped to stand in front of him.

"You've been so concerned with having lost your magic. With the months you spent powerless."

"Of course."

"Well, you weren't powerless. I've never seen anyone fight like you. Your arsenal of potion bombs *are* your magic. You just turned your skill in that direction. I've never met anyone as adaptable and powerful as you."

I blinked like a goldfish, my heart warming at his words. "You've been holding on to this?"

"Been thinking about it, yes." He nodded, his gaze serious. "You were never powerless. You were never down. I wanted to make sure you knew that, because you didn't seem convinced before."

I swallowed hard. "Thank you."

He shrugged, the motion elegant. "It was obvious. I had to say it."

It hadn't been obvious to me, but I didn't mention it. Mostly because I was realizing how close he was. How good he smelled. Cedar and soap, and that indescribably manly scent that I'd come to associate with him.

This close, I could see all the shades of blue in his eyes. The fullness of his lips. Sharp cheekbones. He truly looked like a fallen angel. The type who got into brawls.

The warmth in my heart spread through the rest of me, making me shiver. "Do you want to come up?" The words escaped before I even realized. I wanted to smack my hand to my lips, but I resisted. "For a drink."

A smile tugged at the corner of his lips. "Love to."

As I led him up the stairs, I realized that I didn't really have anything to drink in the house. But then, if I were honest with myself, that wasn't the real reason I was inviting him up.

Did he realize that?

I stepped into my living room, grateful to see that the Menacing Menagerie wasn't here. They would really put a damper on *any* mood.

Maximus followed me in and shut the door. I turned to face him, deciding not to waste any time. I'd run out of courage, anyway. The tension of wanting to kiss him was just too much.

I'd wanted it for centuries, it felt like.

I moved toward him, standing on my toes and pressing my lips to his.

Immediately, he growled low in his throat and pulled me toward him, his strong hands gripping my waist and pulling me up onto my tiptoes. I wrapped my arms around his neck and pressed my body to his, reveling in his warmth and hard strength.

My head spun as we kissed, every inch of me prickling with pleasure. He turned me so my back was pressed against the door. We kissed like that for ages, every moment like a dream.

His scent twisted around me, his touch imprinting on my every cell.

When I thought I might die from the pleasure, a knock sounded at the door, right behind my head.

We both stiffened, our breaths coming fast.

"Oh shit," I muttered.

Maximus pulled back.

I sucked in a steady breath, straightening my clothes and hoping that my cheeks weren't too red. "Want to take a seat on the couch?"

He nodded, his cheeks flushed and his eyes hot. Warmth still raced through me, impossible to banish.

Once he'd sat on the couch, I turned and opened the door.

Ana stood there, brows slightly raised.

Oh fates. Had we been making noises? Moaning, even?

Ana would never let me live that down.

Her gaze moved from me to the living room beyond, landing on Maximus with interest. Her lips quirked up at the corners, and I could tell she was going to demand the details later.

"What is it?" My voice was a weird combo of breathy and snappy, like a pissed-off phone sex operator. I winced, hoping she wouldn't notice.

Ana's smile just got wider. "Lachlan requested a few pieces of your hair. They want to try something different with the potion."

Her words banished every sexy thought from my head, and guilt flooded in.

They were working all night, while I was up here making out with Maximus. It was literally my *job* to sleep and get rest. I was representing the Undercover Protectorate Academy, and if I didn't rest, I wouldn't be strong enough to win.

Shit.

"Of course." I turned and headed into my cluttered kitchen, searching through the masses of stuff on the counter for a pair of scissors. I found them, sitting between a pack of unopened glass globes meant to hold potions and a bag of loose Moroccan clay.

I grabbed the scissors and snipped off a bit of hair, then returned to Ana, who hadn't left the doorway. "Will this do?"

"It should." She smiled. "Now get some rest."

I nodded. "On it.

She left, and I turned back to Maximus. Though my insides still vibrated with pleasure at the sight of him, it was easier to force the thoughts away now. Guilt was a hell of a lust dampener.

"We'd better do as she says. Rest up, and all."

He nodded, standing.

"You can sleep on the couch if you want." I smiled. "If you're lucky, Romeo will join you. Maybe even Poppy and Eloise."

He laughed. "I'm not sure how I'd feel about that, but I'll take you up on the offer."

I nodded. "Help yourself to anything in the kitchen. Which is pretty much nothing."

Before he could speak, I hurried up the stairs. The room was empty, and it didn't take me long to climb into bed. When I finally lay down, my mind was spinning with thoughts of Maximus. Thoughts of tomorrow.

At two p.m. the next day, we gathered on the front lawn of the castle. The sun glinted brightly on the grass and made the windows sparkle. The air was crisp with spring, with just the bite of winter left over.

Jude, Bree, and Ana had come to see us off, but Lachlan was still holed up with Hedy and Connor, hard at work on the potion we hoped they could make.

"Good luck today," Ana said.

"We'll be watching on the mirror." Bree smiled. "Kick ass."

"We have faith in you," Jude said.

I nodded at all three of them, their words warming me. I could do this. I *had* to do this.

After a quick goodbye, Maximus hurled a transport charm on the ground, and we stepped into the glittering gray cloud. The ether sucked us in and spit us out into the bright Croatian sun. I blinked, my eyes slow to adjust.

"We aren't near the water," I said. "So it can't be a boat ride."

"This is the address on the ticket." Maximus turned around. When he was facing the area behind me, his eyes widened. "Well, I'll be damned."

I turned to see whatever had made him curse, and my brows jumped up. "Holy fates."

"Hot air balloon." Maximus whistled. "That seems like a death wish.

"There are four of them." One for each team. The other teams were nowhere to be found, however. Hopefully we'd get a good, solid lead.

Slowly, we approached the balloons, which were rainbow striped and enormous. I dug my ticket out of my pocket and read it. "Berth 1." I looked up, spotting a wooden sign near the balloon on the far right. It was marked with an enormous one. I pointed. "That's our balloon."

By the time we reached it, it was nearly three o'clock in the afternoon. Oliver Keates, the rat-faced representative of the Intermagic Games, stood right next to it.

He smiled and waved. "You're just in time."

"Where are the others?" I asked.

"Delayed. You get a head start since you found the slipper first."

As I'd hoped. I grinned.

He gestured to the balloon. "Better hurry or you'll lose your lead."

I took his advice and picked up the pace toward the balloon, climbing into the big basket. Maximus followed.

Oliver met my gaze. "Any chance you have another one of those vine-killing potions on you? I know my colleague at the Order of the Magica is anxious to inspect it."

I swallowed hard at his tone. There was a bite to it that I didn't like. "Forgot to bring it. As soon as this is over, though, I'll do it."

He nodded, his gaze sharp. "See that you do." He released the lines, and the balloon began to float upward. "The balloon will steer itself. You just have to keep it in the sky."

Keep it in the sky?

Oh, hell. Something was going to attack us. I could just feel it.

Silently, the balloon rose, the air growing colder the higher we got. White wisps floated around our heads, annoying as flies at a picnic. The balloon began to carry us toward the sea, and I leaned over, watching the city glide away below. When I looked back at the balloon field, I caught sight of the two fae approaching their balloon.

"Not much of a lead," I said.

Maximus shook his head, then turned back to face the open ocean. The balloon carried us out over it, the cold wind whipping my hair back from my face.

He squinted into the distance, frowning. "Something is coming."

I joined him, leaning over slightly and trying to see whatever it was. "I don't see anything."

He pointed. "The winged things."

I spotted them, my heart thumping. "The witches?"

Maximus shook his head. "I don't think so. Serpents, maybe. Winged serpents."

I shivered, then dug a hand into my potions bag and pulled out a bomb. "Might as well get ready."

The winged serpents came fast, hurtling toward us through the clear blue sky. They were a pale green color, their scales dull and their wings gray. Four of them screeched toward us, their battle cry making my hair stand on end. Long fangs dripped with venom, and their eyes were onyx crystals.

My heart thundered. These things could knock us right out of the sky if we let them.

I dug into my bag and handed Maximus a couple of potion bombs. "Use these."

I eyed the closest one. It was twenty yards away and gaining speed. I pointed at him. "I've got him."

With precision, I threw my bomb, aiming right for its broad chest. The glass exploded, sending blue liquid splashing down over the beast. It hissed and flailed, clearly about to go down. Then it exploded in a poof of dark magic.

Maximus nailed another one right in the head. Within seconds, it, too, exploded.

I turned my attention to another monster that was closer. I nailed it in the head. It hissed viciously, then poofed away.

Maximus nailed a fourth monster.

This was working, except they were gaining speed. More were coming, and they'd split up, approaching from two sides. In a few seconds, they'd be upon us. Especially the ones that were coming from the right.

Oh, crap.

"I'm switching to a sword for close-range defense," Maximus said. "You take long-range. Your aim is killer."

I nodded. Maximus drew a sword from the ether and

climbed up onto the lip of the basket, holding onto the ropes that attached to the balloon. My stomach dropped at the sight of him hanging out over open sky with a thousand-foot drop below.

I wanted to scream "be careful!", but I bit it back. There was no point. He'd do what he felt like, and he was a pro.

I turned my attention to the serpent that flew toward me. I hurled another potion bomb and took him out. But two more replaced him, appearing right out of thin air. They raced for us, their forms undulating through the air like they were swimming through water.

I dug into my bag as Maximus leaned out with his sword, swiping at the serpent that was close enough to strike.

I threw my potion bomb, missing the one that charged us. *Damn it!* I didn't have a ton of bombs to spare. I dug back into my bag, the edges of my vision catching Maximus as he beheaded the snake. More were coming for him, and he moved quickly.

One after the other, I threw potion bombs, taking out the snakes. My heart thundered in my ears and my breath heaved. There were so many!

We'd never make it.

They were beginning to attack the fae who were a few hundred yards behind us. For every one that the fae blasted out of the air with their glittery blue magic, more seemed to appear, replicating like rabbits after a carrot buffet party.

In the distance, there was a shriek.

My blood chilled. I'd only ever heard that sound from one creature.

I searched the sky, horror dragging me down as I hunted for the witches. That was the sound they made in their bird form.

We couldn't handle another attack. The snakes were more than we could take. And we were right out over the ocean. They couldn't maim with their beaks and claws, but that didn't necessarily mean they couldn't pop our balloon. We were so high that we'd never survive the drop, even with my power over water.

"Do you see them?" I screamed.

"No, but they're so loud that they must be near!" Maximus swung his sword while shouting, taking out two serpents with one strike.

Ice filled me as I hurled my potion bombs at the snakes, continuing to search the sky. Finally, I caught sight of the birds. Two of them, both as massive as I remembered.

They attacked the serpents, unable to pierce them with their beaks or claws but able to drive them away from us.

"What the hell?" I said in a rush.

"What are they doing?" Maximus asked, having finally caught sight of them.

"I have no idea. It makes no sense."

Maximus sliced his sword toward a serpent that was only a few feet away. Blood sprayed as the beast's head toppled toward the sea. A moment later, the whole thing exploded in a poof of foul dark magic. At least they weren't real animals. Just spells.

Because fates, I hated to kill real animals, even mean ones.

Confused, I continued watching the witches as I reached for another potion bomb. I hurled it, taking out a serpent that neared, but I was unable to wrap my mind around what the witches were doing.

"They're protecting us," Maximus said. "Keeping the snakes away."

"They wouldn't turn nice now. I don't buy it." But the proof of his words was in front of my eyes, despite my denial.

"Whoever said it was nice?" Maximus leapt down from his perch on one side of the balloon basket and rushed to the other, leaping up in time to stab a serpent through the middle. "Might be a means to an end."

That made more sense. But what end?

147

Right now, it didn't matter. I had to survive this before I could even think about the witches, and the serpents kept appearing. An insane number. More than I could count.

They focused on our balloon, and there were so many we'd never be able to take them all out. In less than a minute, they'd be on us, a horde of beasts bent on our destruction.

Wasn't that how people in the last competition had died? In a snake pit?

It seemed the Intermagic Games had a thing for snakes and a lack of self-control. Or an inability to decide what was an appropriate number. This right here was *not* an appropriate number.

My heart thundered in my ears as I searched for a way out of this. We were too far from land, and too slow. Not to mention the fact that we didn't know where this balloon was headed. If we wanted to get there, we couldn't abandon our ride.

Panic made my head buzz and my muscles freeze. I'd never felt so trapped before.

A few fluffy clouds floated on the horizon, too far away for us to hide within.

But that was what we needed. A bunch of clouds. Regular white ones to hide us, and vicious storm clouds to drive off the snakes and the witches.

I ached to grab the clouds and pull them toward me. It was a deep, physical pain that was entirely foreign, but so real.

I blinked.

What the hell?

I'd never felt that before.

Magic began to swell in my chest, something new. My connection to the clouds increased, surging within me. When I breathed in, the air felt almost damp. Like *it* was a cloud. Like *I* was a cloud.

Holy fates, what kind of magic was this?

The power surged within me, and the faint cloud that now surrounded us seemed to wobble in the air. All around, serpents flew. The witches swooped in front of our balloon, trying to drive them off, but there were so many. Some of them slipped by, darting right toward us.

Maximus stood on the rim of the balloon basket, holding on to the balloon rope and leaning out to slice at the attackers.

Magic pulsed through me as I tried to reach for a potion bomb, but my hands shook. There was so much of the power in me. It had to be released.

Create the clouds. The voice whispered in my ears, strong and deep. It shook my insides like an earthquake, and I had no doubt that it was a god speaking to me. A god of clouds, or something.

But it made sense, what he said. As the battle raged around me, all I could focus on were the clouds in the distance. On the clouds that seemed to be filling up my soul.

I let the new magic surge inside of me, filling every inch of my being until my skin felt tight. I imagined creating clouds. Shooting them from my fingertips and filling the sky with them.

Finally, it was too much. I released the magic, imagining dozens of clouds filling the sky.

It happened just as I envisioned it, white mist surrounding us immediately.

"I can't see them!" Maximus shouted.

But they were still coming.

A green serpent shot through the clouds and almost slammed into Maximus. He was quick, slicing at the serpent before it hit him in the chest.

But it was too close a call.

Panic flared.

My clouds were backfiring.

These were the wrong kinds of clouds.

I struggled to get ahold of the magic inside me, trying to manipulate it to do my will. I needed a different kind of cloud, and more control over their location.

My limbs trembled as I tried to get control of the magic, gathering it up inside of me.

Rage. Storm. The godly voice kept echoing in my ears, the only directions I was going to get about this new power.

But I took its advice, focusing not only on the magic, but on my rage. Frankly, I was pissed about this whole situation. I liked a bit of danger, but this was over the top. And the snakes were targeting us more than the others.

Eff that.

I stoked the rage, letting it mix with the magic inside me. It gave the power form and direction. The clouds began to turn black. They swirled together, coalescing to form a ring around our balloon. We weren't within the storm, but the snakes now were.

Lightning cracked, the thunder so close that it deafened. Wind whipped through the air, but it was nothing compared to what was pushing the black clouds around in a circle around the balloon. They formed defenses between us and the snakes.

No more snakes lunged out at us. They were trapped in the storm, too busy trying to stay aloft, I imagined.

Maximus turned to me, his eyes wide. He didn't dare speak the words—the wisps were floating all around us—but it was clear that he was asking if I was creating this magic.

I nodded and turned my attention back to the storm. We couldn't keep floating in the middle of it. We had to keep going.

It took all my control to part the storm clouds so our balloon could continue to float. The little contraption bobbed in the air, occasionally shaking from the force of a misplaced blast of wind.

Fates, this was dangerous. My skin chilled. If I lost control of this storm, our balloon would be torn apart, and we'd plummet toward the sea.

My breath came fast as I continued to part the clouds, trying to guess which way the balloon would want to travel. When it got too close to the storm, I parted the clouds in that direction.

Finally, when my muscles were trembling and my magic waning, I let go of the clouds, banishing them and praying that the snakes were all gone.

When the clouds finally disappeared, I blinked.

No more snakes. No more witches in their bird form.

But below us, a massive structure sat in the middle of an enormous city.

The Colosseum in Rome. The massive stone stadium spread out below us, ancient and hulking.

Shock pierced me. I looked up, catching sight of Maximus's pale face.

Clearly, he was thinking what I was thinking.

Oh fates, we were going to fight in the Colosseum.

CHAPTER THIRTEEN

The balloon drifted to a stop on the street outside the Colosseum. It'd been cleared of people, but I could hear the roar of the crowd from inside.

Oliver Keates, along with three other people, ran out from an arch built into the Colosseum's exterior and grabbed onto the balloon basket, reaching for the ropes that lay coiled inside.

I didn't spare him a glance as I climbed out, ready to be away from that damned balloon. My mind raced with memories of the witches. Why had they driven the snakes off? What was their end game?

I wasn't naive enough to think it was good.

"You'll want to reach the main arena as quickly as you can," he said. "Godspeed."

I just nodded and hurried forward, not bothering to speak. Maximus kept pace with me, and I glanced over at his pale features.

"You okay?"

"Fine." His words were curt.

"You don't have to do this, you know." I couldn't imagine the horrible memories he was reliving.

"It's fine." We ducked under the arched entrance into the cool darkness. "Really, it is. I can face my demons."

He was right. If anyone could, it was him. I'd never met anyone stronger.

The Colosseum was shaped like any other stadium I'd ever seen, just super old. We were deep in the bowels of it, with thousands of spectators on the benches that were above us. We stood in some kind of darkened entrance, the old stone illuminated by torches.

"Do you know how to get into the main arena?" I asked.

"From here? No. Let's head right, and I'll get my bearings."

I turned to the right, entering a long hall with tiny rooms on either side. I looked at Maximus, who nodded, his expression dire.

"Holding cells," he said. "We'll keep going through, then to the left. Should be an entrance around there."

My skin prickled as we walked through the darkened corridor. Faint light gleamed from a few torches, but the whole place was cast in shadow and misery.

There were a few benches against the walls, and I spotted some shackles.

"Fuck this place," I muttered. Too much death here. Too much misery.

"Fuck it." Maximus's voice was grim.

I picked up the pace, nearly running through the darkened corridor, not daring to look inside the cells. They were empty—the whole energy of this place was empty and dead—but I wondered if I'd see ghosts if I looked closer.

I didn't want to see Maximus's ghosts.

The next room was actually another corridor, but it had no little rooms off the sides. Just benches with more shackles. Every time I saw a set of them, more rage rose within me. I was starting to feel like one of the storm clouds I'd created outside.

How had Maximus survived this and come out even a little bit normal?

Fates, he had to be strong.

We were halfway down the narrow hall when magic prickled on the air. The white wisps that followed us began to vibrate, almost as if they were excited.

"Something's coming," Maximus said.

My heart thundered. He was right.

The sound of stone scraping against stone made me look up.

The ceiling was dropping.

My skin iced. "The ceiling!"

"Run!"

We sprinted for the end of the hall. As we neared, torchlight flickered on iron bars.

Oh, hell.

I dug into my potion sack, searching for the familiar shape of my disintegration potion. *Please, please be in there.*

Dust and crumbled rock fell down the sides of the walls as the ceiling lowered. I couldn't find the potion I needed! My legs burned as I sprinted full-out, but the bouncing made it hard to find the proper potion bomb.

We were nearly to the door, but the ceiling was so low that Maximus was running in a crouched position. We were about five feet away when he stopped, pressing his hands to the ceiling above. It groaned to a halt.

I spun, catching sight of Maximus's red face and straining muscles.

"I can't hold it long." His voice was rough.

The white lights vibrated around him, the wisps excited by the show. The crowd had to be eating this up.

The thought just enraged me more. Maximus was trapped in the Colosseum again, maybe about to die. All for these people's entertainment.

Death had been a far-off concept when we'd first started this. People talked about those who'd died during the Intermagic Games, but it didn't feel real.

This, though?

This felt real. We were trapped in this temple to misery and pain, where people came to cheer as other people died.

I'd never felt such rage before. It threatened to overwhelm me—like I could just fall over and be consumed by it.

No way in hell.

I had the potion bomb that would get us out of here. Expiring in a fit of rage was literally the worst idea ever. I sucked in a breath and turned, leaving Maximus to hold up the ceiling and praying that he could.

I dug back into my potion bag, my fingertips finally closing around the proper shape.

"Down!" Maximus's grunt was the only warning I got.

I dropped to my knees just as the ceiling creaked and fell lower. A glance back showed that Maximus had been forced to his knees. Veins stood out along his arms and neck, and I realized that he was literally holding up the weight of the whole Colosseum. Like Atlas held up the world.

My heart thundered as I hurled the potion bomb at the metal gate. It disintegrated the metal bars immediately, and I lunged through, turning back to gesture for Maximus. "Come on!"

He let go of the ceiling and leapt, moving so quickly that I almost didn't have time to get out of the way. He hurtled past me, skidding on the stone floor, and the ceiling slammed down in the room behind us.

I turned toward Maximus, shaking. "That was close."

He dragged an arm over his sweaty brow. "Too close."

I stood, inspecting the new room that we were in. Weapons

hung off the wall, axes and swords and pikes. Maximus shuddered, and I reached out to squeeze his arm.

"Miserable place," he muttered, striding through. "We're almost there."

I hurried to catch up, my soul turning blacker with every minute. It was a dark anger, one that filled me up.

When the first weapon on the wall vibrated, I stiffened. "You see that?"

"What?"

I pointed toward the wall, where a sword was vibrating, clattering against the stone.

Maximus cursed, and his magic swelled on the air. A massive shield appeared on his arm, and he shoved it at me. I grabbed it just in time. The sword disconnected from the wall and hurtled toward me. Fast as I could, I held up the shield, which covered me from head to toe.

The sword slammed into the shield, making the metal vibrate and my arm sing. Maximus conjured another shield, and we huddled together, each holding a shield on the side of us that faced the wall.

The weapons began to fly in earnest, swords and pikes and axes hurtling toward us. The white wisps zipped around as the weapons thudded against my shield. Soon, my arm was numb.

When an ax hit my shield with enough force to pierce it, a surprised squeak escaped me. "Let's run!"

We picked up our pace as the weapons continued their assault. One nearly hit my foot, slicing off the very tip of the toe of my boot.

By the time we reached the edge of the room, every inch of me was vibrating from the blows. My ears rang from the sound of metal against metal.

As soon as we passed through the door, the weapons stopped flying. We stopped, dropping our shields in unison and panting. I leaned against the wall, trying to catch my breath.

"Fuck this place," I muttered.

Maximus squeezed my arm, and the human connection grounded me. I opened my eyes and looked around. We were in a wide room with four darkened arches, one on each wall.

Like a horrible gameshow, we had to pick which door. I was certain they were all bad. And if we were delayed much longer, the others would beat us to the arena.

"Do you know which way?" I asked.

Maximus nodded grimly. "To the left. The one across from us also leads to the arena eventually, but it's a longer way. I'd bet it has another deadly obstacle in it."

"Let's skip that."

"My thoughts exactly." He approached the arch on the left, and as he neared it, the gate rose up. Light shined through.

The arena.

We'd made it.

The prize was in there.

But all I could think about were the thousands of people and animals who'd died in this horrible arena over the years. Died so other people could cheer and clap. Disgust welled within me. I didn't know if we'd be walking out into a death battle, but there was no freaking way I was participating.

I looked at Maximus. "Whatever we face out there, I'm not killing the other competitors. And I'm not going to hang around to get killed either. If it's a one-on-one competition, I'm out."

He nodded, his gaze hard.

I reached for his hand, and he gripped mine. Together, we walked through the arch and into the light. It blinded me at first, and all I could hear was the sound of screaming. The crowd, and someone closer. I blinked, my vision adjusting.

There was a fountain in the middle, glowing with blue light

that poured out of it like water. The sun had set while we were trapped inside the corridors of the Colosseum, and I realized that I didn't know how much time had passed. The light that I'd seen when we had first entered came from great torches, which only made this feel like a macabre theatre.

Floating right above the water in the glowing fountain was a golden orb. The pale blue light shined around it, highlighting it.

My gaze darted around the arena, barely processing the full crowd. I only had eyes for the monsters. Three giant ones stood on the far side of the arena. Two were human-shaped, and the other stood on all fours, looking vaguely like a lizard. All vibrated with dark magic, and I'd bet they were straight from hell. Demon monsters.

It was a death trap.

But it was the fourth demon, the one closest to us, that really caught my attention.

He was twenty feet tall if he was an inch. His massive horns speared the night sky, and his arms bulged with muscles. He had one of the blonde illusionists gripped in his fists, just like freaking King Kong. Her blonde hair flew as he shook her.

At the giant's feet, the illusionist's sister beat at his legs with her sword, but it did no good. The blade wasn't strong enough—not against his reinforced skin, at least—and she wasn't a great fighter. She'd relied on her illusions too much. She was either panicking or there was nothing she could show the monster that would make him drop her sister.

I didn't even bother looking back at the fountain and the Truth Teller. We had a straight shot to it. The other contestants hadn't even arrived yet, and the monsters were all the way on the other side of the arena. We could probably race over there and grab the thing right away, but screw that.

I glanced at Maximus, and from the look on his face, he clearly read my thoughts.

"Let's get him," he said.

Together, we sprinted toward the giant.

"I'll take out his legs!" I shouted, drawing my electric sword from the ether. I didn't even bother with potion bombs. This guy was probably too big for any of mine.

"I'll take the neck." Maximus slowed slightly as I sprinted ahead, clearly getting into position.

"Move!" I shouted at the illusionist.

Shocked, she looked up at me, her white eyes widening. I raised my electric sword, and she got the drift, stumbling back.

I sprinted the last few steps toward the demon, who was so obsessed with his King Kong prize that he didn't even notice me. I swung right for his ankle, my sword crackling with power. It severed the foot right off, the electric blade cauterizing the wound.

Maximus roared, and I looked up just in time to see him sail overhead. He jumped so high I gasped, his feet hitting the giant right in the middle. The beast was already wobbly, given that I'd cut off his freaking foot. Maximus's strike sent him flying onto his back.

The gladiator followed him down, stabbing his sword straight into his throat. The giant gasped and gurgled, and his big palm loosened. The trapped illusionist rolled out onto the ground, coughing and gasping.

Maximus jumped off of the dying demon, wiping his sword on the creature's clothes. Any minute now, the bastard would wake up back in hell where he belonged.

Natalia helped Olga to her feet—or maybe it was the other way around, I couldn't tell—and then turned to us. Her white eyes gleamed, and it was impossible to say if it was with suspicion or gratitude. "Why did you help us?"

"I don't want any of us to die. It's a freaking game. No prize is worth that." I looked around at the Colosseum, at the roaring crowd and the three giant monsters who remained. One of them fought the fae, who'd just arrived. The wolves entered the arena next, and one of the giants turned to them. The third giant started to lumber toward us. "If we don't fight together, some of us *will* die."

That snake oil salesman who'd been the announcer had kept saying some of us would bite it. Apparently, they'd planned to *ensure* it.

"It's bullshit," I said. "Death isn't a spectator sport, and this isn't fair. Not against these giants." I looked at Maximus. "Let's go."

I sprinted for the fae, not waiting to hear the illusionists' response.

I didn't need to wait, though.

Natalia's voice echoed after me. "We'll help!"

She and her sister sprinted up to join Maximus and me. Together, the four of us ran toward the fae. They were pinned against the wall of the arena, a huge demon looming over them. He was even bigger than the one who'd gotten ahold of the illusionist, and he wore armor from neck to feet. A massive helmet covered his head but allowed his horns to poke through, piercing the sky.

The demon threw fire at the fae, who darted left and right, avoiding the blasts with their quick speed. They wouldn't manage it forever, though. Even now, they were slowing.

Imani, the woman, raised her hands, and a blue, glittering cloud burst forth. Birds flew amongst the cloud, their beaks sharp and eyes bright. They charged the demon, flying up toward his head and going straight for the eyes. They were quick, their aim good.

The demon roared, raising his hands to cover his eyes and swat at the birds.

Hell yeah!

Another demon appeared. The third one—the one who'd been coming toward us earlier. Human-shaped, also wearing massive armor. He raised a hand and hurled fire at the fae, seeming to enjoy ganging up on the little guy.

Bastard.

Jabari, the male fae, created another cloud of glittering devil birds. But the giant was ready. His helmet came equipped with a visor, and he snapped it down over his eyes.

"We'll shield you!" Natalia shouted.

Ahead, a dozen fae appeared. Jabari and Imani replicated over and over again. The giants roared, clearly confused. They didn't know which ones to strike. They might not even realize that they were illusions. They were way more brawn than brains, definitely.

We were nearly to the demons, and I searched for a weak spot. Somewhere that wasn't covered by armor. My gaze snagged on the giant's neck where a piece of leather connected the helmet to the breastplate.

There.

I pointed. "Maximus! Can you boost me up there? Then you can take the other one out."

He nodded and put on some speed, racing ahead of me. The demon was still swatting at the birds and didn't notice Maximus kneel behind him, making a cupped shape with his hands.

I stashed my electric sword in the ether and sprinted ahead, then placed my foot in Maximus's palms. He heaved me upward, and I flew through the air and grabbed onto the demon's waist. He was huge, and the armor was covered in scales, giving me good handholds.

Below, Maximus disappeared into thin air.

The illusionists. It had to be. They'd made him invisible. Hopefully I had the same treatment.

I began to climb up the giant's back. He thrashed and roared, clearly realizing that I was there.

When his big hand slapped backward, I didn't even see it coming. I felt it, though, when it crushed me against his armor.

Pain flared in my middle. I gasped, agony shooting through me. Broken ribs? I clung tight to the demon's back, pain radiating as I tried to breathe shallowly. *Breathe through the pain.*

The giant continued to thrash, trying to throw me off him, but I started climbing, trying to move as quickly as I could. My ribs ached with every movement, but I focused on the job.

Finally, I reached the giant's neck where the leather was creased and soft. I held on with my left hand and reared back, calling my electric sword from the ether. It appeared in my right hand, and I stabbed, sending the blade right into the giant's neck. He roared, stumbling.

Oh fates, I hoped he fell on his front.

From below, the faes' magic surged. I caught sight of the blue sparkles out of the corner of my eye and looked down. They slammed their magic into the demon's back, sending him careening onto his front.

Heck yeah. They kept me from becoming a pancake on his back.

The giant slammed to the ground, and I bounced, my ribs aching.

As quickly as I could, I scrambled to my feet, searching for Maximus. I couldn't see him, but the giant demon that he'd presumably jumped onto was thrashing in the air, blood spurting from his neck.

Maximus had to be landing a killing blow, and a big part of me was satisfied to know that because of the illusionists' invisibility magic, the bloodthirsty crowd had missed most of the action.

A second later, Maximus appeared, hanging on to the giant's

back just like I had. The fae raced forward, hitting the giant in the back with their magic so he fell onto his front and didn't crush Maximus.

I sprinted over.

Jabari and Imani turned to me.

"Thanks," they said in unison.

I nodded. Maximus climbed to his feet, looking pretty whole. I was having a hard time breathing with my ribs, but at least I was standing.

In the distance, the two wolves fought the giant lizard. They were doing pretty well—considering that they weren't yet dead —but their thick brown coats were covered with slices that leaked blood. The lizard had mean claws, long and sharp. Clearly, he knew how to use them.

I sprinted for the lizard, Maximus joining me. Footsteps thundered behind us, and I glanced back to see that the fae and the illusionists were coming to help.

Everyone ignored the stupid Truth Teller and the fountain. I didn't know how the crowd was taking this development, but they could go screw themselves.

We reached the lizard just as he swatted one of the wolves with his front limb, sending the wolf flying straight into the arena wall. The other wolf crouched low, growling, getting between his fallen brother and the lizard.

Once again, the fae pulled their multiplication trick. A dozen wolves appeared, then a wall of flame, separating the growling wolf from the lizard. Through the flickering fire, I caught sight of the main wolf—at least, I thought it was him—turn and lope toward his fallen brother.

I sprinted toward the lizard, running side by side with a glittery cloud of the blue birds. The fae sent their attack birds toward the lizard's face while I leapt onto its back and stabbed my sword deep.

The lizard reared up on hind legs, hissing wildly. I fell off and slammed to the ground. The beast stepped on me, one razor-sharp claw slicing through my left forearm. Pain flared.

I screamed, unable to help myself, then scrambled upright. The lizard had fallen back down, and Maximus had leapt onto its back. He stabbed the creature through the back of the neck, but it didn't go down.

Crap.

Imani, who stood closer to the Colosseum wall, hurled a blast of magic at the lizard's back legs. The cloud slammed into his limbs, and the right one went limp.

The same trick that had frozen that poor butler and my arm.

I wasted no time in climbing up onto the lizard's back again, though my movements were slow and awkward. Blood dripped from my wounded arm. I raised my blade and plunged it down. The beast shrieked and reared up on his only good leg, throwing me toward the center of the arena.

I hit hard, pain flaring in my ribs, and skidded in the dirt.

When he fell, he slammed to the ground and lay still.

I must have hit his heart. It was hard to tell on a demon, but the monster was definitely dead.

Maximus had been thrown off toward the Colosseum wall, but he was rising to his feet. Imani and Jabari stood near the body. The illusionists were only about fifteen feet from me, their hands outstretched and their magic flowing toward the fight. They let their fire die. The wolves had both stood.

The monsters were gone.

The fight was over.

Everyone looked alive. Beaten up, but definitely alive.

I looked back at the fountain and the Truth Teller.

I was the closest one. Not by a lot, but with the battle over...

Before I could even turn, the other contestants sprinted

toward me, their eyes on the prize that was about thirty yards behind me.

I turned and raced for it as well, my chest aching like I was being stabbed by a dozen knives. I called upon the cloud magic within me, commanding the fluffy white things to fill the arena. I wouldn't bring down the lightning or the winds—no way would I hurt the other competitors—but making it hard to find the fountain didn't sit too wrong with me.

The illusionists were fast, though. I caught sight of them out of the corner of my eye. Ahead of me, six fountains appeared.

The damned multiplication trick. But I'd been running right toward the proper fountain, and it was still the one that was right in front of me. If I just kept on course, it'd be the right one. I hoped.

I pushed myself, running faster than I ever had in my life.

This competition was a whole load of bullshit, but I still wanted the prize. The Undercover Protectorate could do so much good with it. The idea was heady. And I wanted to know what pantheon I represented. What kind of Dragon God I was.

The thought gave me strength, and I ran faster. The white clouds filled the stadium, blocking us from the viewers. My lungs burned and sweat poured as I ran.

Somehow, despite the pain that raced through every inch of me, I pulled ahead of the illusionists. They hissed, but I kept going, giving it everything I had. When my hand pushed through the glowing blue light that surrounded the golden Truth Teller, I felt a prickle of protective magic. Then my fist closed around the golden orb, and I pulled it free.

Victory surged through me.

I'd won.

From overhead, dark magic swelled. Confused, I looked up, just in time to see one of the witches swooping down toward me in her bird form, her huge claws outstretched for me.

165

Horror welled in my chest.

She reached me a half second later, scooping me up in her massive claws but never piercing any of my skin. She swooped high, heading for the sky with me gripped in her claws. Wind tore through my hair as I watched the Colosseum disappear into the distance down below.

Holy fates, I was screwed.

CHAPTER FOURTEEN

Cold wind tore through my hair as the giant bird carried me through the air. The city whipped by below, golden lights traveling fast. At first, I thrashed, trying to break free. Then I stilled, heart thundering in my ears.

What the heck was I thinking?

The last thing I needed was to fall. I couldn't freaking fly, after all. And I could try to drive the birds out of the sky with my cloud magic, but then I might *still* fall. We were so high up that I'd be a pancake for sure if it let me go.

So I lay limp in the bird's claws, heart thundering and body aching. They were bound by magic to prevent them from using their beaks and claws to hurt people, but apparently carrying people around like dolls was still allowed.

Carefully, I craned my neck to look down, my eyes watering from the chill wind. My stomach plummeted as I checked out the view below, but I didn't recognize anything.

Where the *hell* were we going?

Everything in my body hurt—the broken ribs, the sliced arm. It was becoming hard to hold on to the Truth Teller, as well, my hands turning numb from the cold. Honestly, with the way my head was spinning, I wasn't sure I could stay conscious.

Carefully, I tucked the Truth Teller into an inner pocket in my jacket. The thing was only half the size of a baseball, so it fit easily.

Once it was stored safely away, I tried to get to a healing potion in my belt, but it was too hard to reach. The way she had me gripped made it impossible to touch my comms charm as well, so I couldn't call my sisters.

Weariness spread over me as the bird flew, carrying me along. The bird was beginning to descend when my consciousness finally started to fade away. As my vision blackened at the edges, I realized that *this* was why the witches had saved us from the flying serpents. There had been a protection charm around the Truth Teller. That glowing blue light had probably been enchanted to only allow a real contestant to grab the thing. That was the Intermagic Games's solution, and it had sucked.

Consciousness came slowly, and only because I had to pee *really* badly. Not to mention the agony that raced through my arm and ribs.

I blinked groggily, staring up at the ceiling. The room was entirely dark. The ground hard.

Why was I sleeping on the floor? That was a terrible idea. I must have fallen off the bed and hurt my ribs and arm.

Aching, I sat slowly and reached for the lamp that would be on the bedside table above me. My hand met open air.

What're you doing?

Romeo's voice snapped my attention down to my lap, where I hadn't felt the weight until now. The raccoon sat on my thighs, eyes concerned within his black mask. Eloise sat at my hip, petting it gently, while Poppy sat on my legs, staring intently at me.

"Where am I?" Because clearly, I wasn't at home like I'd thought.

The bird women brought you here. Romeo began to poke at my belt. *You need a healing potion.*

"The birds?" Oh, shit. I'd forgotten. Those witches had picked me up at the Intermagic Games and carried me away.

Frantic, I patted my jacket, looking for the Truth Teller. There was no telltale lump under the leather, and when I stuck my hand into my pocket, it came up empty. "Shit."

Romeo kept poking at my belt, and he had a point. Every inch of me ached. With trembling hands, I reached for the little vial on the right that would contain a healing serum. I shook my hand to ignite the magic on my lightstone ring and inspected the vial, just to make sure.

It shined in the light, opalescent and lovely.

Yep. Healing potion.

I took a quick swig, sighing as the pleasure raced through me. It wasn't real pleasure, but honestly, the feeling of pain fading away was close enough.

"Where am I?" I asked.

Greece, again. I think. Smells like it.

I sniffed the air, only able to pick up on the scent of the sea and dry desert ground and maybe some kind of vegetation. Romeo had always said he had a good sniffer, though.

Gently, I shoved him off of me. Poppy hopped off of her own volition, and I stood, feeling better than I had in ages. That healing potion worked quickly, and I was grateful I'd taken the time to pack it.

I raised my lightstone ring to inspect the room while I pressed my fingertips to my comms charm. "Ana? Bree?"

"Rowan! We're coming to get you!" Bree's voice sounded.

"Your tracking charm is giving us some trouble," Ana said. "Where are you?"

"In a little building." I inspected it through the glowing light of my ring. "About fifteen feet by fifteen feet. One tiny window on each wall. Greek writing on the ceiling."

I wished I could read it, but that wasn't ever going to happen. I walked to the nearest window and looked out. "Sea on one side." I walked to the next window. "Hills on the other."

"We're on one of the hills," Bree said. "We got close, but the magic in your tracking charm is a bit blocked."

"We'll be right there," Ana said. "I've got a visual from the air."

Thank fates for the tracking charm.

"Is Maximus okay?"

"He's with us. He's fine," Bree said. "Sit tight. We'll be there soon."

I went to the door and tried it, but of course it was locked tight. The windows were way too small for me to fit through.

I looked at Romeo. "Did you see where the women went?"

Down the hill, up another hill. There's a temple there. You can't miss it.

I nodded. "Thanks. You guys should get back. It's not safe here."

Eloise scoffed. Poppy tittered disapprovingly.

As if we'd leave you!

"Thanks, guys."

I searched the room for my potion bag, but couldn't find it. The witches must have figured out it was full of weapons and taken it. Dang.

I dug into my belt and found my highly concentrated disintegration potion. The same one I'd used to break out of the pit at El Dorado.

The lock on the door was big and old, solid iron. Carefully, I poured the liquid onto it and watched it sizzle. Within seconds, the lock was gone.

You could break into any kind of dumpster with that!

I grinned back at Romeo. "I'll keep that in mind."

Carefully, I pushed the door open, ready for a guard to jump out. None did, and my shoulders sagged in relief. It was still night, though the moon was getting low on the horizon. Dawn could arrive soon.

The sea glittered on one side of me, with rolling hills all around. A massive white temple sat on top of one of the hills, pale blue magic glowing from the roof. The witches would be in there, using the Truth Teller for whatever evil shit they had planned.

Quickly, I found a bush and took care of business. When I stood, I searched the sky, spotting two winged figures flying toward me.

A giant crow and the silver-winged Valkyrie. I raised my hand and waved, but didn't shout. They landed a few moments later. Bree grinned widely. Ana shifted to human form and was smiling as well.

"I knew you'd break yourself out." Ana threw her arms around me.

Bree joined in, squeezing me hard.

I hugged them tight, then pulled back. "Where's Maximus?"

Bree turned around to look toward one of the other hills that was farther away from the temple. "He should be coming any second. We followed the tracking charm, but it led us to another hill."

"It was close, at least," Ana said.

A moment later, Maximus crested our hill, clearly having run from another one. His expression relaxed as soon as he saw me, and he strode over. "Are you all right?"

"I'm fine."

He hugged me tight, and I squeezed him back, then turned to Ana and Bree. "Where are Cade and Lachlan?"

"Lachlan's still working on that potion," Bree said. "Cade is hunting an ingredient. They might almost have it. Let's get out of here, and hopefully they'll be done."

"We can't go yet."

"What?" Surprise sounded in Ana's voice.

"The witches are still here." I pointed to the temple. "In there."

Ana shoved her hand through her blonde hair. "Damn it. Too much to hope they'd drop you and run."

"They took the Truth Teller. I think they waited until I grabbed it because only a contestant could reach through the protection charm on the fountain."

"Fates." Maximus frowned. "There's no telling what miserable things they are learning from it."

"We have to stop them," I said.

"We could wait for backup," Ana said. "But I have a feeling you won't like that idea."

I shook my head. "Not so much, no. We can't give them any more time with the Truth Teller. Let's do it now."

My sisters nodded, then turned to face the temple. We started off at a swift jog, the Menacing Menagerie keeping pace easily.

This was like a mirror of our first adventure in Dartmoor. Running down one hill and up onto another, seeking the danger within the building that sat on top.

It wasn't until we reached the shallow valley between the hills that I felt the first prickle of awareness. Dark magic seeped out of the ground, sticky and nausea-inducing.

"Something is coming." I pointed ahead, low to the ground.

"I feel it," Maximus said.

The earth rumbled, a great roar that shook my legs. In front of us, the earth rose up, piling over itself to form two great beasts. They looked like wolves built from dirt, their fangs made of stone and their eyes a glowing black onyx.

"That's some spell," Ana breathed.

The wolves had to be forty feet tall if they were an inch. When they began to run, the earth trembled beneath their feet. Dirt poured off them, only to be reabsorbed back through their paws.

"Our weapons won't work on them," Maximus said. "They're just dirt."

"I've got this." Bree flew up high, her magic swelling on the air. Lightning shot, bright and fierce, plowing into the nearest wolf. Thunder followed, cracking in my ears, but the wolves kept running, totally unaffected.

"They aren't alive," I said. "I don't think we can kill them by normal means."

They pounded closer, only sixty yards away now. Maybe less. Cold fear prickled my skin.

"Let me try." Ana held out her hands, her magic flaring. She could use her Druid magic to control the earth, and she was clearly trying to influence the wolves. They kept plowing toward us, though, their footsteps shaking the ground. Ana grimaced and sweat dripped down her temple, but nothing changed.

"It doesn't work." She lowered her hands.

The wolves were nearly upon us.

"Better run," Maximus said.

I sucked in a deep breath, getting ready. Then we sprinted. We split up, darting different directions to confuse the wolves. The Menacing Menagerie ran circles around them. But they were smart and fast.

The wolves rampaged, trying to stomp us into the dirt. One of them nearly got me once, the vibrations of his footsteps through the ground almost sending me to my knees. Bree and

Ana took to the sky, trying to distract him, but it didn't work. Every blow they landed had no effect.

Shit, *nothing* was working.

My heart thundered and my muscles ached as we tried to outrun the beasts, but they kept blocking us from the temple.

How the heck was I going to stop them?

I eyed the ocean. At first, I'd thought it was too far, but I was desperate enough to try.

I reached for the water with my magic, straining because it was so far off. I could barely feel it. I pushed harder, trying to call the water to me. Sweat dripped down my back. Finally, I caught hold of it. I forced a plume of water to rise up from the ocean and rush toward us.

"Clear out, Maximus!" I shouted. "You too, Menagerie!"

They all darted away from the wolves. Bree and Ana did the same. I sprinted to the right, and the wolves followed. It took everything I had to send the blast of water right at them. It sprayed me in the face as it plowed into them and turned them to mud. They collapsed, washing away in a tidal wave of thick brown sludge. It piled up around my boots and then my knees.

Oh fates, it was *deep*.

Maximus and the Menacing Menagerie had sprinted toward the temple, so they were out of the way of danger, but it was rising higher and higher around me, dragging at me, trying to pull me under.

My heart thundered and my skin turned to ice.

Panic tightened my throat as I looked up.

Ana swooped down toward me, her black crow form glinting in the light. She got as low as she could, and I reached up and grabbed onto one of her curled talons. She pushed her wings hard, soaring upward and plucking me out of the mud.

We sailed over the river of sludge, and she dropped me on

the upslope of the next hill, right next to Maximus. I panted, propping my hands on my muddy thighs.

"Nicely done," he said.

"It was close." I straightened.

My sisters landed next to me. We were only about forty yards from the temple. Dark magic rolled out from it, and the roof glowed brighter than ever.

"Let's go." I started up the hill, running as quickly and silently as I could, though our cover was probably blown.

As we approached the temple, it loomed tall above us. Massive white columns supported the huge roofs. When five minotaurs stepped out from behind the columns, each at least eight feet tall and wielding a broadsword, I didn't even slow. Though I did wish I had my potion bombs.

I pulled my electric sword from the ether and charged the nearest minotaur. His ugly bull face was adorned with horns and fangs, and pure evil glinted in his black eyes.

Oh yeah, these guys were from hell all right.

Minotaurs were just an ancient breed of Greek demon, and I wondered how the witches had enlisted them. They were notoriously hard to hire.

Bree's lightning cracked through the air, while Ana dived down in her crow form to attack with her claws. Maximus swung his sword, going head-to-head with two minotaurs. The Menacing Menagerie had ganged up on one minotaur, with Poppy going for the eyes while Eloise struck for the throat. Romeo had leapt onto his head, where he beat at the minotaur's skull.

I lunged for the one nearest me, swiping out with my blade. He dodged backward, but I followed, fast and determined. Whatever was happening inside that temple, I had to stop it.

The beast sliced at me with his wide blade, the steel glinting wickedly. I darted right, but too slowly. The thing sliced me across the thigh, and blood welled.

I ignored the pain, lunging again and going for his throat. I was too short, and the tip of my blade cut a bright red line across his chest. He roared, swiping out with his claws, and I danced backward. As he raised his sword to strike again, I put on a last burst of speed and sank my blade into his stomach.

His eyes widened, and he made a gurgling noise. I grimaced and yanked my blade out, letting him fall backward onto the stairs.

Maximus had taken out his two minotaurs, and a few other bodies lay scattered, courtesy of Ana and Bree. No guards were left standing, so I charged up the stairs. Maximus kept stride with me, and my sisters followed.

Bree landed on the stairs, folding in her silver wings, while Ana shifted from crow to human, racing up alongside us. The Menacing Menagerie climbed swiftly, their eyes alert and tails raised high. The huge entryway to the temple was open, revealing a massive space.

Before we stepped through, I leaned down to Romeo. "Stay away from the danger, but grab the Truth Teller if you can. It looks like a golden egg. Then get out of here."

He nodded his little head, his black eyes determined.

"And remember," I said. "If it gets too dangerous, bail."

All three animals scoffed, ignoring me.

I stepped into the temple, taking it all in.

In the middle, a massive dark cloud rose up. The two witches stood around it, their black hair floating eerily around their heads. I squinted at the vision in the cloud, only able to make out terrifying black mountains and lightning. What were they looking at? There was clearly more detail in the image, but I couldn't see it from here.

A loud hiss from the right side of the temple broke their

concentration, and they whirled to glare at us. I looked between them and the animal that had made the hissing noise.

A massive eight-headed snake slithered toward us, glittery green eyes glued on my sisters. Bree's silver wings sprouted from her back, and she burst into the air, her sword raised. She flew right for the snake and sliced out with her blade, cleanly removing one of the heads.

She swooped away, avoiding the other striking heads. Within seconds, the head that she had severed grew back as two more.

"Crap! A Hydra!" How the hell were we going to kill it?

A memory of the battle at the Colosseum flashed through my mind. Of me, slicing through the giant's leg with my electric blade. A blade like that might cauterize the wound, making it impossible for two heads to grow back.

I drew the sword from the ether and shouted, "Ana! Catch!"

She turned, her eyes wide. I tossed the sword to her, and she caught it by the hilt.

She nodded. "On it!"

Next to her, Maximus conjured his own sword. "I'll distract it while Bree and Ana go in for the kill."

Ana tossed the blade to Bree, who was still hovering in the air. She darted toward the Hydra, then sliced out with her blade and removed a head.

I didn't stick around to see if it worked. If it failed, I was sure I would hear about it. And I was certain that ignoring the witches would be a *real* bad idea.

I turned to face them. The dark image had fallen away from behind them, revealing the golden Truth Teller, sitting alone on a pedestal.

The witches glared at me, their purple eyes flashing and their hair floating around their heads. They rose up on their tiptoes, some kind of dark magic helping them to float across the floor as their tattered gray dresses dragged behind them. A shiver rolled down my spine.

As they raised their hands, dark magic crackled. I swallowed hard, waiting to see what they would send at me. When the bright orange flame burst forth, I lunged backward.

They sent it roaring toward me, a wave of fire. From behind them, I could see the Menacing Menagerie creeping toward the Truth Teller.

Excellent. I just had to stay alive and keep everyone else alive while they did that.

The fire was a problem, though. It rushed toward me as a wall, hot and fierce. This was no illusion. I dived left, narrowly avoiding it. On the far side of the temple, my sisters and Maximus battled the Hydra, which was presumably the witches' bodyguard. If they could just keep it off me long enough...

I called upon my magic, reaching for the sea. I'd douse their flame with the ocean.

But the ocean didn't respond.

It was too far away.

Definitely too far away.

Shit.

Panic sent my heart racing. The wall of flame was closing in on me, encircling me. The heat was insane, almost driving me to my knees.

I needed water. Something to douse it with.

The clouds.

The idea popped into my head. That might work. I called upon my new magic, focusing on the image of a cloud in my mind. I called upon a rainstorm, forming a massive cloud right overhead. It was hard at first, the magical equivalent of pulling teeth. But the cloud grew and grew.

The flames grew and grew, too.

They were nearly to me when the clouds finally released

their downpour, snuffing out the flames. Steam rose around me, almost as hot as the fire itself. I curled into a ball, protecting my face.

When it faded, I jumped up, my throat burning from the heat. I squinted through the steam, finally catching sight of the witches.

They drifted closer to me, floating along on their toes, their purple eyes glinting with evil.

"What *are* you?" I screamed.

Twin smiles stretched across their faces. "We are the Stryx, and we are here to claim what is ours."

"What the hell does that even mean?" Fear and rage coiled within me.

They raised their hands and sent a blast of magic at me. I dived left, but it was too fast. Too strong.

The sonic boom plowed into me, throwing me back against the ground. My head spun as I gasped, trying to catch my breath. I felt like my insides had been pulverized.

I couldn't see them, but they had to be coming closer.

Aching, I dragged myself to my feet. The witches were nearly to me, still floating creepily in the air. They raised their hands again, ready to smack me with another blast.

The idea just pissed me off. I wasn't their plaything.

Electric anger filled me, making me vibrate with rage. It surged through my chest, filling my limbs. I shook with it, so hot and pissed that I felt like *I* was a lightning bolt.

Energy crackled from me, and I felt my hair stand on end.

The witches' purple eyes widened, shock paling their faces.

Hang on...

I looked down at myself, realized that I actually *was* crackling with energy. Electricity shot up and down my arms, bright and bold.

Holy crap, I was a human lightning bolt.

I looked up, then charged, sprinting toward the witches as fast as I could. The one on the right acted quickly, throwing up her hands and creating a white force field.

I plowed right through it, spreading out my arms so I slammed into both witches. The shock made them screech. It also tore through me, pain lighting me up.

We tumbled to the ground in a pile. They shook from the electricity, but I couldn't hold on to them for long. It hurt too badly for me as well.

I yanked my arms back and curled in on myself, aching all over. The witches rolled away from me, scrambling to their feet. I forced myself to rise, to follow them, but they were too fast.

They shifted back into their winged forms and launched themselves into the air, then swooped out through the wide doorway.

Panting, I stared after them.

They'd decided to cut their losses and run. Or they'd gotten what they'd wanted from the Truth Teller.

Aching, my lungs heaving, I turned in a circle. On the far side of the temple sat the Menacing Menagerie, Eloise clutching the Truth Teller proudly. On the other side were my sisters and Maximus. Bree chopped off the last Hydra head, and Maximus kicked the thing in the chest, sending it flying backward. The monster slumped against the wall, headless, then disappeared in a poof of black magic.

The temple went silent.

I stood, exhausted, and surveyed my companions. Wounded, but standing upright. I considered that a big victory. They staggered over to me. The Menagerie followed, and Eloise handed the Truth Teller to me.

I leaned down and took it, the heavy weight cool in my hand. "Thanks, guys."

They nodded, looking tired. Their fur was a bit singed in places.

"I couldn't hope for better sidekicks."

That got me three toothy grins.

"Where'd the witches go?" Ana asked, her right hand pressed to a wound on her left arm.

"I don't know." I sat down hard on the marble floor, no longer quite able to hold myself upright. "Apparently I'm a human lightning bolt, and they didn't want a hug."

"A hug?" Bree choked on a laugh.

"Yeah. I give terrible hugs." I lay back on the floor and stared up at the ceiling. "Anyone know what a Stryx is?"

"No," Ana said. "But I bet we can find out."

"Good, because I think that's what we're fighting. And I think they got what they wanted from the Truth Teller, too."

"That sounds like very bad news." Maximus sat next to me. He draped his arm around my shoulders, his expression concerned.

"I think it is."

CHAPTER FIFTEEN

We arrived back on the Protectorate lawn about thirty minutes later. It'd taken me a while to recover from the electricity trick I'd pulled, and I still had no idea how I'd done it.

Finally, Maximus had had to drag me up off the ground. Even now, I leaned against his shoulder as we stumbled up the lawn. Bree and Ana walked alongside, followed by the Menacing Menagerie.

"Thanks for coming, guys," I said.

Bree grinned widely. "Wouldn't miss it."

"It was a challenge this time." Ana chuckled, as if she'd enjoyed that bit. "I thought we might be done for when the flame came, but you got us out of it."

"Barely."

"That's all you need, sometimes," Maximus said.

We stepped through the grand entry into the castle and pulled up short. Panic surged briefly in my chest.

Right there, in the middle of my home, stood the cocker spaniel from the Order of the Magica and rat man from the Intermagic Games. Harry Ward and Oliver Keates. They stood with Jude, who looked at them with serious eyes.

Shit.

They were going to want that potion that withered the vines. Just to make sure *I* wasn't the one with the creepy death magic. Seriously, could I not get a break for just a half second?

As if they'd heard the door open, the three of them turned to look at us.

"Ah, the woman of the hour herself." Harry Ward grinned, but it wasn't pleasant.

"Back from absconding with the Truth Teller?" Oliver Keates said.

"Absconding?" I gave him my best *eat-shit* expression. "I was abducted, you moron. By the same interlopers I told you about. They wanted the prize."

Oliver's eyes widened. "But we protected it!"

"Only until one of the contestants grabbed it." I couldn't help but snap. "And since you put us in that creepy Colosseum, it was open to the sky, and I was yanked out of there by a giant freaking bird."

"But...but..."

I didn't let Oliver finish. "I think you need to seriously rethink the nature of the Intermagic Games. That was just meant to be a disgusting death show."

"It raises the stakes," he said weakly.

"Screw your stakes."

Harry Ward cleared his throat. "All of those issues aside, it seems that you are fine now. Did you recover the Truth Teller?"

"I did, no thanks to you."

He nodded, clearly annoyed but putting on his best business face. "In that case, perhaps you could show us the potion that you used to steal the life from the vines back on Dartmoor? You know, just crossing our t's and dotting our i's. Can't have any Magica with unknown death powers running around."

A chill snaked through my hot anger. I was about to bluff about needing a moment to recover, but Jude cut in.

"Perhaps you should just run and get that, Rowan. Get this whole messy business over with. It's in your room, isn't it?"

My gaze darted to hers, and I couldn't read her expression. Then again, in iffy circumstances, Jude would never give away the game.

I had to trust her.

Or run for it, once I reached my room.

I nodded curtly. "Fine. I'll go do that."

Maximus helped me walk away, but I did my best to lean away from his strength. As much as I appreciated it, I was pissed. And when I was pissed, I liked to stomp off on my own. Unfortunately, my stomping was a little pathetic given that I was still shaky from turning into a human lightning bolt, but I felt better for trying.

As soon as we were up the stairs and out of earshot, Maximus leaned in. "Do you actually have this potion?"

"No. And I don't know if my friends are finished making it. Last I heard, they hadn't succeeded."

"So you could be making a run for it?"

"Could be." The idea sent a streak of fear down my spine.

Maybe I wouldn't have to run for it *right* away. Maybe I could buy some time. Unless Jude was sending me up here because she knew they'd never find a way to make that potion, and my chances were up.

My breathing came faster and my skin chilled at the idea. I slowed as I walked down the hall to my room, afraid of what I might find. When I turned the corner and spotted Connor laying a package down in front of my door, I stopped dead.

"Connor?" My voice wavered.

He stood, a grin on his face. His Imagine Dragons T-shirt

covered in sparkly potion residue. Quickly, he thrust the box toward me. "All done."

My heart leapt. "Really? You made it?"

"We just finished."

I ran over and hugged him, so grateful I could cry. My friends had my back, thank fates. They'd worked so hard to save me. It made me just as happy as the idea of handing over the potion and getting the Order of the Magica out of my hair..

Connor pulled back. "Well? Are you going to go give it to them?"

"Right now." Relief surged through me. "This is all over. Almost."

I turned to grin at Maximus, happiness welling within me. Thank fates for friends.

Maximus and I hurried back down the hall. The cocker spaniel and the rat were waiting in the main entry hall, both of them tapping their foot impatiently. Bree and Ana stood on either side of them, watching them warily, as if they'd have to jump on them and hold them down while I ran away.

Thank fates for my sisters.

I strode up to them and handed them the potion. "Here it is."

Harry Ward gave the potion vial a skeptical look as he took it.

"It'll work," I said, totally confident in my friends' ability.

"We'll see." He tucked the vial into his pocket. "We'll get back to you soon with the results of our test."

I nodded, since there was nothing else I could say.

Oliver Keates stepped forward. "Congratulations on winning the competition. The audience enjoyed the show." I scowled at him, and he shifted uncomfortably. "Normally, there would be a ceremony at the end, but as you disappeared after collecting the Truth Teller, we won't be having one."

"Good." Because I wouldn't show up anyway. The last thing I wanted was to be under the microscope again, especially now that I'd gotten what I wanted and there was no reason.

Oliver nodded. "We'll be going, then."

We said our goodbyes and watched them leave. Thank fates that was all over.

"You look like you've been through the wringer," Jude said.

I turned to her and nodded wearily.

"Let's get some food." She gestured to the stairs leading down to the kitchen. "Then we can talk."

"Yes." The word came out of me almost as a moan. But damned if I couldn't sit down and get a bite to eat.

Jude, Maximus, my sisters, and I all trooped down to the kitchen, where Hans had a big vat of soup waiting. The steam curled up from the massive pot, smelling of vegetables and herbs. My mouth watered, distracting me from the ache in my muscles.

Hans turned to us, his mustache quivering in delight. "Guests! Sit, sit!"

I collapsed into a chair at the scarred, round table, absorbing the warmth from the fire that crackled nearby. The Menacing Menagerie sat in front of it, eating from plates that looked like they'd been filled at the compost bin. Romeo gave me a toothy smile. I smiled back, weariness stretching through me.

In moments, Hans had big steaming bowls in front of us, along with juice boxes. Always with the juice.

"Thanks, Hans. You're the best." I dug in gratefully.

After the first few bites, I leaned back and looked at Jude. She was waiting for me to speak, and I appreciated her patience.

"So, we didn't catch the witches." I pulled the Truth Teller out of my pocket and set the golden egg on the table. "But we have a clue about what they are." I recounted the battle to her, including the scene that the Truth Teller had created.

"So they're after something big," Jude said.

I nodded.

"That's what we think," Maximus said. "They've got a plan, and they're slowly putting it into place. They didn't go after Rowan or me when they had the chance. They're after something bigger."

"We need to make sure they don't get it." Jude picked up the Truth Teller. "Well done, Rowan. This will help us in our work. I can't even tell you how much. The lives we'll save with this..."

I smiled, glad to have been able to bring it back here.

She held the Truth Teller up so it glinted in the light. "For this, you'll advance to the next level at the Academy. You're moving just as quickly as your sisters. Maybe quicker."

I smiled, shocked. But it was Bree and Ana who smiled even bigger.

"According to Oliver Keates, the Truth Teller doesn't have unlimited uses," she continued. "It needs to recover after each use. But I thought you might want to use it to figure out what Dragon God you are."

I grinned, nodding. "I'd like that."

She set the egg on the table. "Well done, Rowan."

Three nights after the Order of the Magica had reported back that the potion had worked and that they deemed I didn't possess death magic—morons—I stood with my sisters in my living room.

"Are you ready?" Bree asked.

I looked down at the Truth Teller. It sat in my hand, heavy and golden. The light gleamed off the surface, and I sucked in a slow breath.

"I'm ready."

LINSEY HALL

Ana nodded and stepped back from the center of the room. I laid the Truth Teller down on the floor, then stepped over to join her. She gripped my hand. Bree joined us and took my other hand.

My heart raced as I considered how to ask my question. A dozen options flashed through my mind, but I went for simple. "What kind of Dragon God am I? What pantheon is giving me their powers?"

Magic swirled up from the Truth Teller. I breathed deeply as it rolled over me, sending a shiver down my spine. A glittery cloud rose up and coalesced to form an image.

Clouds rolled in front of me, filling the room. A figure appeared, misty at first. They stepped through the clouds, approaching.

Bree and Ana squeezed my hands.

Immense magical power rolled toward me. It blasted the breath from my lungs and made me sag. I kept myself upright—barely—and blinked.

The figure wore a simple white tunic trimmed in gold that matched his shining hair. Golden sandals with wings glinted at his feet.

I gasped, my mind catching on a long-ago memory of a mythology book. Those sandals...

"Hermes?" I asked.

An enigmatic smile pulled at the edge of his mouth, and he held out a scroll. Trembling, I reached out to take it. My skin prickled as soon as I touched the heavy paper. As I unrolled it, Hermes stepped back into the clouds, disappearing.

"That was quick," Bree murmured.

My head buzzed as the scroll revealed the text within. The language was ancient, the letters foreign. But as I stared at it, they began to make sense, as if my brain were rewiring to understand the ancient language.

"I'm the Greek Dragon God." I looked up at Bree and Ana, shock nearly freezing my tongue. "Apparently, I've got the powers of Zeus."

THANK YOU FOR READING!

I hope you enjoyed reading this book as much as I enjoyed writing it. Reviews are *so* helpful to authors. I really appreciate all reviews, both positive and negative. If you want to leave one, you can do so at Amazon or Goodreads.

Join my mailing list at www.linseyhall.com/subscribe to stay updated and to get a free ebook copy of *Death Valley Magic,* the story of the Dragon God's early adventures. Turn the page for an excerpt.

EXCERPT OF DEATH VALLEY MAGIC

Death Valley Junction
  Eight years before the events in Undercover Magic

Getting fired sucked. Especially when it was from a place as crappy as the Death's Door Saloon.

"Don't let the door hit you on the way out," my ex-boss said.

"Screw you, Don." I flipped him the bird and strode out into the sunlight that never gave Death Valley a break.

The door slammed behind me as I shoved on my sunglasses and stomped down the boardwalk with my hands stuffed in my pockets.

What was I going to tell my sisters? We *needed* this job.

There were roughly zero freaking jobs available in this postage stamp town, and I'd just given one up because I wouldn't let the old timers pinch me on the butt when I brought them their beer.

Good going, Ana.

I kicked the dust on the ground and quickened my pace toward home, wondering if Bree and Rowan had heard from Uncle Joe yet. He wasn't blood family—we had none of that left besides each other—but he was the closest thing to it and he'd been missing for three days.

Three days was a lifetime when you were crossing Death Valley. Uncle Joe made the perilous trip about once a month, delivering outlaws to Hider's Haven. It was a dangerous trip on the best of days. But he should have been back by now.

Worry tugged at me as I made the short walk home. Death Valley Junction was a nothing town in the middle of Death Valley, the only all-supernatural city for hundreds of miles. It looked like it was right out of the old west, with low-slung wooden buildings, swinging saloon doors, and boardwalks stretching along the dirt roads.

Our house was at the end of town, a ramshackle thing that had last been repaired in the 1950s. As usual, Bree and Rowan were outside, working on the buggy. The buggy was a monster truck, the type of vehicle used to cross the valley, and it was our pride and joy.

Bree's sturdy boots stuck out from underneath the front of the truck, and Rowan was at the side, painting Ravener poison onto the spikes that protruded from the doors.

"Hey, guys."

Rowan turned. Confusion flashed in her green eyes, and she shoved her black hair back from her cheek. "Oh hell. What happened?"

"Fired." I looked down. "Sorry."

Bree rolled out from under the car. Her dark hair glinted in the sun as she stood, and grease dotted her skin where it was revealed by the strappy brown leather top she wore. We all wore the same style, since it was suited to the climate.

She squinted up at me. "I told you that you should have left that job a long time ago."

"I know. But we needed the money to get the buggy up and running."

She shook her head. "Always the practical one."

"I'll take that as a compliment. Any word from Uncle Joe?"

"Nope." Bree flicked the little crystal she wore around her neck. "He still hasn't activated his panic charm, but he should have been home days ago."

Worry clutched in my stomach. "What if he's wounded and can't activate the charm?"

Months ago, we'd forced him to start wearing the charm. He'd refused initially, saying it didn't matter if we knew he was in trouble. It was too dangerous for us to cross the valley to get him.

But that meant just leaving him. And that was crap, obviously.

We might be young, but we were tough. And we had the buggy. True, we'd never made a trip across, and the truck was only now in working order. But we were gearing up for it. We wanted to join Uncle Joe in the business of transporting outlaws across the valley to Hider's Haven.

He was the only one in the whole town brave enough to make the trip, but he was getting old and we wanted to take over for him. The pay was good. Even better, I wouldn't have to let anyone pinch me on the butt.

There weren't a lot of jobs for girls on the run. We could only be paid under the table, which made it hard.

"Even if he was wounded, Uncle Joe would find a way to activate the charm," Bree said.

As if he'd heard her, the charm around Bree's neck lit up, golden and bright.

She looked down, eyes widening. "Holy fates."

Panic sliced through me. My gaze met hers, then darted to Rowan's. Worry glinted in both their eyes.

"We have to go," Rowan said.

I nodded, my mind racing. This was *real*. We'd only ever

talked about crossing the valley. Planned and planned and planned.

But this was *go time*.

"Is the buggy ready?" I asked.

"As ready as it'll ever be," Rowan said.

My gaze traced over it. The truck was a hulking beast, with huge, sturdy tires and platforms built over the front hood and the back. We'd only ever heard stories of the monsters out in Death Valley, but we needed a place from which to fight them and the platforms should do the job. The huge spikes on the sides would help, but we'd be responsible for fending off most of the monsters.

All of the cars in Death Valley Junction looked like something out of *Mad Max*, but ours was one of the few that had been built to cross the valley.

At least, we hoped it could cross.

We had some magic to help us out, at least. I could create shields, Bree could shoot sonic booms, and Rowan could move things with her mind.

Rowan's gaze drifted to the sun that was high in the sky. "Not the best time to go, but I don't see how we have a choice."

I nodded. No one wanted to cross the valley in the day. According to Uncle Joe, it was the most dangerous of all. But things must be really bad if he'd pressed the button now.

He was probably hoping we were smart enough to wait to cross.

We weren't.

"Let's get dressed and go." I hurried up the creaky front steps and into the ramshackle house.

It didn't take long to dig through my meager possessions and find the leather pants and strappy top that would be my fight wear for out in the valley. It was too hot for anything more, though night would bring the cold.

Daggers were my preferred weapon—mostly since they were cheaper than swords and I had good aim with anything small and pointy. I shoved as many as I could into the little pockets built into the outside of my boots and pants. A small duffel full of daggers completed my arsenal.

I grabbed a leather jacket and the sand goggles that I'd gotten second hand, then ran out of the room. I nearly collided with Bree, whose blue eyes were bright with worry.

"We can do this," I said.

She nodded. "You're right. It's been our plan all along."

I swallowed hard, mind racing with all the things that could go wrong. The valley was full of monsters and dangerous challenges—and according to Uncle Joe, they changed every day. We had no idea what would be coming at us, but we couldn't turn back.

Not with Uncle Joe on the other side.

We swung by the kitchen to grab jugs of water and some food, then hurried out of the house. Rowan was already in the driver's seat, ready to go. Her sand goggles were pushed up on her head, and her leather top looked like armor.

"Get a move on!" she shouted.

I raced to the truck and scrambled up onto the back platform. Though I could open the side door, I was still wary of the Ravener poison Rowan had painted onto the spikes. It would paralyze me for twenty-four hours, and that was the last thing we needed.

Bree scrambled up to join me, and we tossed the supplies onto the floorboard of the back seat, then joined Rowan in the front, sitting on the long bench.

She cranked the engine, which grumbled and roared, then pulled away from the house.

"Holy crap, it's happening." Excitement and fear shivered across my skin.

Worry was a familiar foe. I'd been worried my whole life. Worried about hiding from the unknown people who hunted us. Worried about paying the bills. Worried about my sisters. But it'd never done me any good. So I shoved aside my fear for Uncle Joe and focused on what was ahead.

The wind tore through my hair as Rowan drove away from Death Valley Junction, cutting across the desert floor as the sun blazed down. I shielded my eyes, scouting the mountains ahead. The range rose tall, cast in shadows of gray and beige.

Bree pointed to a path that had been worn through the scrubby ground. "Try here!"

Rowan turned right, and the buggy cut toward the mountains. There was a parallel valley—the *real* Death Valley— that only supernaturals could access. That was what we had to cross.

Rowan drove straight for one of the shallower inclines, slowing the buggy as it climbed up the mountain. The big tires dug into the ground, and I prayed they'd hold up. We'd built most of the buggy from secondhand stuff, and there was no telling what was going to give out first.

The three of us leaned forward as we neared the top, and I swore I could hear our heartbeats pounding in unison. When we crested the ridge and spotted the valley spread out below us, my breath caught.

It was beautiful. And terrifying. The long valley had to be at least a hundred miles long and several miles wide. Different colors swirled across the ground, looking like they simmered with heat.

Danger cloaked the place, dark magic that made my skin crawl.

"Welcome to hell," Bree muttered.

"I kinda like it," I said. "It's terrifying but..."

"Awesome," Rowan said.

"You are both nuts," Bree said. "Now drive us down there. I'm ready to fight some monsters."

Rowan saluted and pulled the buggy over the mountain ridge, then navigated her way down the mountainside.

"I wonder what will hit us first?" My heart raced at the thought.

"Could be anything," Bree said. "Bad Water has monsters, kaleidoscope dunes has all kinds of crazy shit, and the arches could be trouble."

We were at least a hundred miles from Hider's Haven, though Uncle Joe said the distances could change sometimes. Anything could come at us in that amount of time.

Rowan pulled the buggy onto the flat ground.

"I'll take the back." I undid my seatbelt and scrambled up onto the back platform.

Bree climbed onto the front platform, carrying her sword.

"Hang on tight!" Rowan cried.

I gripped the safety railing that we'd installed on the back platform and crouched to keep my balance. She hit the gas, and the buggy jumped forward.

Rowan laughed like a loon and drove us straight into hell.

Up ahead, the ground shimmered in the sun, glowing silver.

"What do you think that is?" Rowan called.

"I don't know," I shouted. "Go around!"

She turned left, trying to cut around the reflective ground, but the silver just extended into our path, growing wider and wider. Death Valley moving to accommodate us.

Moving to trap us.

Then the silver raced toward us, stretching across the ground.

There was no way around.

"You're going to have to drive over it!" I shouted.

She hit the gas harder, and the buggy sped up. The reflective surface glinted in the sun, and as the tires passed over it, water kicked up from the wheels.

"It's the Bad Water!" I cried.

The old salt lake was sometimes dried up, sometimes not. But it wasn't supposed to be deep. Six inches, max. Right?

Please be right, Uncle Joe.

Rowan sped over the water, the buggy's tires sending up silver spray that sparkled in the sunlight. It smelled like rotten eggs, and I gagged, then breathed shallowly through my mouth.

Magic always had a signature—taste, smell, sound. Something that lit up one of the five senses. Maybe more.

And a rotten egg stink was bad news. That meant dark magic.

Tension fizzed across my skin as we drove through the Bad Water. On either side of the car, water sprayed up from the wheels in a dazzling display that belied the danger of the situation. By the time the explosion came, I was strung so tight that I almost leapt off the platform.

The monster was as wide as the buggy, but so long that I couldn't see where it began or ended. It was a massive sea creature with fangs as long as my arm and brilliant blue eyes. Silver scales were the same color as the water, which was still only six inches deep, thank fates.

Magic propelled the monster, who circled our vehicle, his body glinting in the sun. He had to be a hundred feet long, with black wings and claws. He climbed on the ground and leapt into the air, slithering around as he examined us.

"It's the Unhcegila!" Bree cried from the front.

Shit.

Uncle Joe had told us about the Unhcegila—a terrifying water monster from Dakota and Lakota Sioux legends.

Except it was real, as all good legends were. And it occasionally appeared when the Bad Water wasn't dried up. It only needed a few inches to appear.

Looked like it was our lucky day.

~~~

Join my mailing list at www.linseyhall.com/subscribe to continue the adventure and get a free copy of *Death Valley Magic*. No spam and you can leave anytime!

AUTHOR'S NOTE

Thank you for reading *Hunt for Magic!* If you've made it this far, you've probably read some of my previous books and know that I like to include historical places and mythological elements in my stories. Sometimes the history of these things is so interesting that I want to share more, and I like to do it in the Author's Note instead of the story itself.

Hunt for Magic was so much fun because I got to include quite a few places that I love. Edinburgh Castle, for one, though I did make some adjustments to the architecture. I added a tall crenelated tower to one side of it, as well as the toilet chute through the wall. This is a common type of toilet in medieval castles and I added one to Edinburgh Castle. I don't believe they have one exactly as I described it, but it was too good not to include.

On Dartmoor, when Rowan is running down the hill toward the haunted house, she notices a huge ring of large stones. This is meant to be Grimspound, a late Bronze Age settlement that was built and occupied around 1450–700 BC. It consists of a circular stone wall surrounding twenty-four smaller stone circles that were once houses. Dartmoor is full of amazing prehistory, and I wanted to include a little bit when Rowan went to visit.

The other main historical element in the book is the Colosseum in Rome. It is a fascinating place, but also a tragic place. Though I love the two places mentioned above, I don't actually love this one. The history is just too awful (and I'm fairly certain I made my feelings clear in the book). I invented the crazy rooms underneath the stadium seating, but the real Colosseum is also full of corridors and passages, some of which even go underneath the main fighting arena.

I think that's it for the history and mythology in *Hunt for Magic*—at least the big things. I hope you enjoyed the book and will come back for more of Rowan, Maximus, Ana and Bree!

To Mary and David, with love.

ACKNOWLEDGMENTS

Thank you, Ben, for everything. There would be no books without you.

Thank you to Jena O'Connor and Lindsey Loucks for your excellent editing. The book is immensely better because of you! Thank you to Aisha Panjwaneey, Erin T., Richard Goodrum and Eleonora for you keen eyes with spotting errors.

Thank you to Orina Kafe for the beautiful cover art. Thank you to Collette Markwardt for allowing me to borrow the Pugs of Destruction, who are real dogs named Chaos, Havoc, and Ruckus. They were all adopted from rescue agencies.

ABOUT LINSEY

Before becoming a writer, Linsey Hall was a nautical archaeologist who studied shipwrecks from Hawaii and the Yukon to the UK and the Mediterranean. She credits fantasy and historical romances with her love of history and her career as an archaeologist. After a decade of tromping around the globe in search of old bits of stuff that people left lying about, she settled down and started penning her own romance novels. Her Dragon's Gift series draws upon her love of history and the paranormal elements that she can't help but include.

COPYRIGHT